BURN FOR YOU

A SMALL TOWN ROMANTIC SUSPENSE

KAIT NOLAN

For Susan,
Because you love the underdog.
Love,
Kait

A LETTER TO READERS

Dear Reader,

This book is set in the Deep South. As such, it contains a great deal of colorful, colloquial, and occasionally grammatically incorrect language. This is a deliberate choice on my part as an author to most accurately represent the region where I have lived my entire life. This book also contains swearing and pre-marital sex between the lead couple, as those things are part of the realistic lives of characters of this generation, and of many of my readers.

If any of these things are not your cup of

tea, please consider that you may not be the right audience for this book. There are scores of other books out there that are written with you in mind. In fact, I've got a list of some of my favorite authors who write on the sweeter side on my website at https://kaitnolan.com/on-the-sweeter-side/

If you choose to stick with me, I hope you enjoy!

Happy reading!

Kait

CHAPTER 1

I t's just drinks.

But as she stepped out of her car, Delaney Newell smoothed her sweaty palms over the skirt she'd worn like she was on an actual date.

No. I wore a skirt like a girl who likes skirts.

Never mind that she hadn't actually *done* that in years. She did like skirts. When she wanted to look nice and show off her legs. It was just… there had been nobody she'd wanted to do that *for* in a long time. Nobody except Sean Murphy, her study buddy and the object of the deep and embarrassing crush she didn't have the courage to do anything about. The gorgeous, sexy firefighter, who hadn't seen her as anything but a classmate. Or so she'd thought until he'd asked her out for drinks to celebrate the completion of their EMT certification.

She'd said yes. Of course she had. And then she'd spent the last few hours working herself up to an absolute dither, analyzing what the hell it meant. Was it just a friendly gesture or was it more?

It doesn't mean anything.

But oh, Delaney wanted it to mean something.

It's not going to mean a damned thing if you don't march yourself through that door to meet him.

She didn't see his truck, but the parking lot of The Mudcat Tavern was packed, and the overflow stretched on down the street. For just a moment, she quelled at the idea of walking in, alone, in front of all those people. The very notion of so many eyes on her made her physically ill. The stares and the whispers—and the not whispers—had dropped off over the past several months. It wasn't like it had been. But it still went against the grain to do anything that potentially drew attention to herself.

It's busy. Nobody will notice you.

She'd gotten good at making herself invisible over the past couple of years.

Squaring her shoulders, Delaney went inside. For a night without live music, the bar was unusually busy. The chalkboard hanging in the entryway announced *Beat the heat! $2 Pitchers,* with a list of beer brands underneath. That would do it. The August heat was still oppressive, even this close to sundown. The roar of conversation pressed down on her as she made a slow circuit, scanning tables and booths for Sean without actually meeting anybody else's eyes. After two laps through, she admitted the truth. He wasn't here.

He didn't stand you up.

For all her lack of confidence, Delaney knew Sean well enough to be certain of that. He wasn't cruel. If he wasn't here, it was because he got delayed. Maybe he caught a fire. The Wishful Volunteer Fire Department had been hopping with the drought conditions hanging over this part of Mississippi since May.

She checked her phone for a text. Nothing. Well, she was obnoxiously punctual, so maybe he was running a little late. She'd just get something to drink at the bar while she waited. Slipping through the crowd, she found a little open spot and bellied up to the long, polished stretch of wood. Adele Daly, the owner of The Mudcat, moved like a whirlwind behind it, pouring shots and pulling pints as if she had six arms.

"What can I getcha?"

Delaney started to just order water. But on the off chance that Sean wasn't able to make it, she didn't want tonight to be a total waste. She'd come out to celebrate. "Whatever hard cider is on tap, please."

By the time she had the drink in her hand, there was still no Sean. After a few moments' debate, she sent a quick text saying she was here. If he was running late, maybe that would prompt him to say so. Although, if he was still at a fire, he certainly wouldn't be checking his messages.

Delaney sipped at her cider and wished she didn't feel so ill at ease. Maybe she should've talked one of her girlfriends into coming as a buffer. Just in case. Not that the list of possibilities there was long. Most of her so-called friends had dropped her, and she'd cut herself off from most of the rest. Keisha would've come, but Delaney remembered she had that out-of-town wedding this weekend. And anyway, she hadn't wanted a buffer in case this was actually supposed to be a date.

"Why Delaney Newell, don't you look a picture?"

Her shoulders tensed at the oh-so-familiar voice. This was not the easy drawl she'd been expecting. This was the stuff of nightmares. Ruthlessly forcing herself to move slow and steady—the picture of unaffected—Delaney sipped at her cider and turned. "Hello, Bryce."

Her ex made a slow perusal of her body,

from head to toe and back again, lingering on the legs bared by the skirt she now regretted wearing. Once upon a time, she'd have found such attentions flattering. Once upon a time, she'd loved him. That had been Before. Now that hungry look just made her skin crawl. His smile spread, slick and oily. Had he always had this creeper vibe, and she just hadn't seen it?

"Want some company?"

"I really don't." She couldn't even regret the bite to her tone.

"Oh now, don't be like that."

"I'm waiting for someone."

An expression of *yeah sure* flickered over his face. "I just wanted to talk."

"I have nothing to say to you." *Please, please let Sean get here soon.*

"I know we didn't part on the best of terms."

"You cheated on me. And unless something's changed, you're still with Gina."

Bryce dialed up the sleazy smile. "She never has understood me as well as you did."

This man represented the worst time of her

life. She didn't want him back. Didn't want to associate with him. She didn't want anyone to even see them together because that would just start the gossip engines up anew. She'd worked too hard and too long to overcome all that.

Seeming to realize his current tack wouldn't work, Bryce shifted gears. "You've been doing well for yourself. I heard you went back to school."

Delaney's fingers pressed so hard against her glass, she wondered the thing didn't shatter. "Why do you care?"

"I always cared about you, sugar. And I just wanted to say how proud I am of what you've done with yourself the past couple of years."

He'd destroyed her life, and now that she'd started to get everything back together, he was sniffing back around? Words, harsh and hateful, clogged in her throat. But she didn't let them fly. That would make him too important and giving them voice would draw too much attention to herself and the situation. With a dawning horror, she watched him reach out a hand to brush the hair from her cheek. She wanted to stumble back, not to let those fingers skim over her skin. He didn't have the right to touch her anymore. But with shoulder-to-shoulder patrons, she barely had room to move. Warring with the cringe was an equally strong desire not to cause a scene. As her instincts battled, her feet remained rooted in place, and she understood that despite the bar full of people, she was utterly alone, with no one here to save her.

SEAN WAS LATE. Almost unforgivably so. Wishful wasn't even big enough to blame it on getting caught in traffic. Well, unless there was some kind of funeral procession. Which there hadn't been. He'd spent way too long at county headquarters, going over the map he'd been maintaining of the fire threats in the region and trying to convince the powers that be to take an offensive rather than defensive position in the face of the months-long drought. The best he'd managed was to get the boss man to temporarily reinstate use of the fire towers to watch for threats. It was a minor victory, but he'd take it.

The interior of The Mudcat was loud. Exactly the kind of atmosphere Sean knew Delaney hated. He hoped she hadn't given up on him and bailed already. It'd be a damned shame to blow it now, after all those months he'd spent coaxing her out of her shell. His eyes scanned the throngs of people, searching her out. There, on the other side of the bar. The dark red hair that had been haunting his dreams shone in the dim lights. His automatic smile froze as he realized she wasn't alone. Some guy was all up in her personal space, reaching out a hand to touch her. Every muscle of her body was poised to flinch away, but she didn't move, seeming frozen like a deer in the headlights. This guy was the kind of asshole who wouldn't back off without a fist to the face or some other guy pissing to mark his territory. Since he didn't think Adele would appreciate a bar fight, Sean went with Plan B.

Cutting through the crowd like a hot knife through butter, he reached Delaney's side in a half-dozen strides, inserting himself between her and the douchebag, as if he hadn't seen the guy reaching for her, hadn't been able to see anything but her.

"Hey, babe."

He caught the flash of relief and gratitude in her eyes, the confusion at the endearment, then saw the flare of surprise when he didn't simply stop. Riding on instinct, he slid his hand beneath the fall of that hair, tipped her face up to his, and kissed her.

Sean meant it to be just a gentle peck. Something chaste, like a high school freshman at the end of his first date. But the moment his lips touched hers, Delaney gasped. Her mouth opened under his and Hercules himself wouldn't have been able to resist taking just a little taste. He got a hint of sharp apples and spice, like an apple pie. Sean freaking loved apple pie.

For one beat—two—he waited to see if she'd push him away. Instead, Delaney's body, which had been straining away from the other guy, melted into him, her hand coming to his chest before skimming up over his shoulder to curve around his nape. His body was giving a whole lot of *Hell yeah*. And then she sighed—a contented purr of a sound that absolutely did him in and made him forget they were in a very crowded bar and this was about proving a point to somebody else.

It was the cheer and wolf whistle that pulled him back, had him lifting his head.

Delaney's big blue eyes slowly blinked open. Her pupils were blown wide, and her kiss-swollen lips parted in a way that had him wanting to taste her again.

There was a reason he shouldn't be doing that. Sean was sure of it. While he waited for his brain to finish rebooting, he just said, "Hi."

"Hi."

God, he liked knowing he'd caused that slightly breathless tone.

"Sorry I'm late." Remembering why he'd started this, Sean shifted, sliding an arm around her waist as he turned toward the douchebag. "Is this guy bothering you?"

Delaney cleared her throat. "He was just leaving."

Douchebag eyed him with considerable hostility. Sean just arched a brow in a *You-wanna-try-me?* gesture. Years of wrangling fire hoses and hauling other heavy equipment meant Sean easily had an extra thirty pounds of muscle on the other man.

Douchebag took a step back, gaze shifting to Delaney. "I'll see you around."

"No, you really won't. You lost whatever shot you had with me a long time ago, and as you can clearly see, I've moved on. Get lost, Bryce."

Sean pulled her a little closer and flashed a smug smile at Bryce to back up her words. Nostrils flaring, he turned away. Sean didn't budge, watching as the guy moved through the crowd and straight to the exit, metaphorical tail between his legs. Good.

As soon as Bryce was out of sight, Sean reluctantly let Delaney go.

She was looking everywhere but at his face, and spots of color flew high on her fair cheeks. "So, um… not that I'm not grateful for the assist but… why did you do that?"

Damn it, he'd embarrassed her.

"Sorry about that. I saw him bothering you when I came in. His type doesn't back off just because a woman asks, and that seemed to be the most expedient means of shutting him down that wouldn't end up with me getting arrested for assault."

"Oh. Well, thank you?" It came out more of a question than an expression of gratitude, and she was frowning somewhere in the vicinity of his left shoulder.

Sean told himself to leave it there and say something to get them back on even footing. To the friends they'd slowly become over the past several months. But then he thought about how she'd kissed him back.

"And at the risk of coming off like an opportunistic asshole, I also did it because I've been thinking about it for the last four months."

Her head snapped up at that, those eyes going wide with surprise, that kissable mouth dropping into an O.

Sean offered a rueful smile. "I guess inviting you out tonight was not as obvious a clue in that direction as I'd originally thought." He'd played things so slow and close to the vest, apparently, she hadn't even realized. *Great job, Murphy.*

The blush got deeper. "I didn't want to make assumptions. I... months? Really?" A timid, hopeful smile curved her lips.

Sean relaxed. He hadn't blown it. "Really. Let me buy you that drink and I'll tell you about it."

He hunted up a table in the corner, one where she could sit largely out of view. Over the months he'd hung out with her, he'd learned she was pretty uncomfortable in public. He'd never asked why and wasn't sure if it was some kind of social anxiety or something else. But he didn't want her to be any more nervous than she already was.

Once they'd put in an order for their drinks and an appetizer sampler, Sean leaned forward in his seat, lacing his hands together on the tabletop. "I have a confession to make."

One delicate brow winged up. "Another one?"

"Well, it's part of the first. I didn't actually have to take the EMT course."

Delaney frowned. "But I thought you had to be recertified."

"I did. But recert courses tend to be much shorter. They're refreshers, not the whole en-chilada. I took the whole thing over again to hang out with you."

"That seems… kind of extreme."

Too late, Sean wondered if that made him look like some kind of stalker. It had seemed like a good idea at the time. "I didn't mean it in a creepy way."

She laughed. "No, I mean, that seems like an expensive and time-consuming option. Why didn't you just ask?"

"Oh. Well, honestly, I thought you might bolt. You're shy. Getting to know you in a group context through school stuff seemed like it'd be less threatening."

Something that might've been consternation flickered over her face and was gone. "God, you're a sweetheart. I've never felt threatened by you, Sean." In a tone so low he could barely hear it, she muttered, "I know what it is to be threatened."

Yeah, he'd been afraid of that.

When he'd been a kid, he and his brother, Collin, had found a dog out at the baseball field a couple miles from their house. It had been skinny as a rail, with a thin whip of a tail, and ears that seemed permanently lowered. After begging and pleading with their parents, they finally got permission to bring the dog home.

But it had taken weeks to coax it close enough. And even years later, Flash had been skittish around strangers, hunching into shadows and hiding whenever somebody came over. Delaney reminded him of that dog. There was a deliberation to her attempts to be invisible, and he wondered what she was hiding from. But tonight wasn't the time for asking about it, so he let the comment slide.

"While we're in confession mode, I have one to make myself." Delaney dropped her gaze again, rubbing a finger up and down through the condensation on her glass.

Sean couldn't stop thinking about what that would feel like on him. Shifting in his seat, he dragged his attention firmly to her face. "Oh, yeah?"

"I took that bow hunter safety course back in January to spend time with you."

"Really? How did you even know I was taking it?"

She jerked her shoulders, still not meeting his eyes. "That day you were at the clinic for your physical, I overheard you talking to Eli about it."

"We'd just met. You didn't even know me yet."

The color was up in her cheeks again. "You kinda rescued me that day, when I almost dropped the vials from that bloodwork in the hall. Our patient has terrible veins and blood-work is always hard on her." The look on her face was far more serious than a simple catch seemed to warrant. Then she banished it with a smile that skated the edge of flirty. "Besides, have you looked in a mirror?"

He flashed a grin. "I was too busy looking at you that day." At her look of skepticism, he added, "No, really. You had your hair all twisted up with those stick things, and they slipped when you dropped the vials. Your hair came half down around your shoulders."

She snorted in self-derision. "I was a mess that day."

"You were gorgeous." He'd spent the rest of that week wondering what she'd look like with all that red hair loose and mussed from his hands. He hadn't known her then. The desire had only grown stronger over the months he'd spent working his way under that careful shell.

She was still blushing, but now it seemed underscored with a glow of pleasure. Sean vowed to make it a priority to elicit that glow on a regular basis. He lifted his glass. "To confessions. And getting out of our own way."

Did he imagine that shadow crossing her face? Surely it was a trick of the light.

With her first truly honest smile of the night, Delaney lifted her glass and clinked it to his. "Cheers."

CHAPTER 2

"Okay, we've covered inventory, appointments, and general concerns." Shelby Abbott, the clinic office manager, made a last sweeping check mark on her list. "Do we have any new business?"

At this, every single member of the staff, including Delaney's boss, Dr. Miranda Campbell, turned to look at her, brows raised in expectation.

They know.

Delaney's gut clenched at the idea, though she shouldn't be surprised. Sean hadn't exactly been subtle with that display at The Mudcat Friday night. Despite the fact that they'd spent the last few nights talking into the wee hours in that glorious, giddy, get-to-know-each-other binge of a new relationship, she wasn't keen to advertise it. The more people who knew they were involved, the more likely someone would explain to him exactly why he shouldn't date her. Sean didn't know about her past. She'd have to tell him at some point, but right now she just wanted to enjoy the simplicity of being liked for who she was by a guy who'd always treated her as a normal person.

So, she played dumb. "What?"

"You're *sure* there's nothing you wanna tell us?" Keisha asked.

Inspiration struck. "Oh! Well, I finished my EMT certification on Friday."

Piper Stewart, the other nurse, clapped her hands. "That's wonderful!"

Miranda pulled Delaney into a quick, side-arm hug. "I'm so proud of you. What's next?"

"I've hardly had time to think about it."

Which was true. She'd spent all the last three days thinking about Sean. And his mouth. And those hands.

"Well, you know you have a place here as long as you want it," Miranda assured her.

"That means more to me than I can say." Delaney swallowed against the knot in her throat. Miranda had given her a chance when no one else would. She owed the woman everything.

Keisha crossed her arms. "Sure there's nothin' else?"

"Maybe something about a certain firefighter?" Behind her lime green cheaters, Shelby's eyes danced with avid interest.

"I thought he was with the forestry service," Piper said.

The truth was Sean was both. Not that Delaney was getting into that with them. She spread her hands. "I have nothing else to say."

"Delaney Newell?"

She spun on her perch atop Shelby's desk to see a veritable explosion of tiger lilies through the open glass of the partition. "Yes?"

The bouquet shifted, and a woman's head appeared. "Delivery for you."

"Um." They were too big to accept over the desk. She skirted her coworkers—avoiding their eyes—and opened the door to the waiting room.

The delivery woman handed over the massive vase. "Enjoy."

"Thank you." Flummoxed, Delaney only stood there, staring at the flowers as the woman left. Had anyone ever sent her flowers before? There'd been that one measly pink carnation her high school boyfriend had sent during the Dollar Flower Drive their sophomore year, but she hardly thought that counted. Certainly, nobody had ever sent her anything so beautiful as this riot of color.

"Well?" Shelby demanded. "Who are they from?"

Setting the vase on the front desk, Delaney plucked out the card.

Confession: Thinking of you.
Your not-so-secret admirer.

There was no stopping the instant bloom of a smile. He'd sent her flowers. For no reason at all. And he'd done it right, sending them to her workplace, where they could be shown off, which was the entire point of sending a woman flowers. Of course, she didn't want to show anything off, but Sean wouldn't know that.

"Oh now, I gotta know who put that smile on your face," Keisha insisted.

Delaney rolled her eyes, but the semi-permanent grin took all the potential sting out of it. "Okay, fine. Sean."

"I *knew it!*" Keisha pumped a fist in the air. "Malika Hobbs saw him laying a big one on you at The Mudcat on Friday."

Her and near to a hundred other people. There was no telling who else had heard by now.

"He was saving me from my ex. As grand gestures go, it was a good one. And I guess we're kinda dating now." Delaney shrugged when what she really wanted to do was burst into The Macarena.

"Well, I think it's awesome," Miranda announced, as the office door opened, and the first patients of the day began pouring in. "And further discussion will have to wait. Time to hop to, y'all."

After taking a moment to clip the stamens out of the blooms in the name of protecting anybody with allergies, Delaney left the flowers on the front desk so everyone could enjoy them as they went through the day.

Between their regular patients and the annual physicals for Brister Construction, everybody was rushing. Delaney even got pulled from her usual post in the back, handling insurance and payments—anything involving computers—to direct patients.

"Mamie Landon?"

A middle-aged woman with a towering helmet of *I-Love-Lucy* red hair rose from her seat. "Why, those flowers are just lovely. Who's the lucky lady?"

"That would be me," Delaney admitted.

"Oh?" The woman's expression sharpened like a dog on scent. "Who's your beau?"

Before she could think of a way to put the question off, glass shattered. Delaney whirled to see Gina Draper standing by the front desk, the vase at her feet. With an ugly sneer, the other woman stomped on the beautiful blooms. The waiting room had gone silent, and Delaney wished for the floor to open up and swallow her as the other half of the worst mistake of her life marched across the room.

"How dare you?" Gina demanded, waving the card from the flowers.

"What?"

"How dare you use your skanky ways to try to lure him back? Bryce is mine. Don't you be thinking you can sink your claws back into him."

Shocked and more than a little frozen under the attention of everyone in the waiting room, Delaney could barely speak. "What the hell are you talking about?"

"People saw you with him Friday night. 'Not so secret admirer' my ass."

"Then people are blind. I wasn't *with* Bryce. He hit on me, and I shot him down." With a massive assist from Sean, but she didn't want to bring him into this right now lest Gina get it into her head to say something to him about it. "The flowers are not from him."

"Oh please," Gina scoffed. "You have never gotten over losing him. You've never been able to accept that he's mine."

Delaney struggled for calm. "Listen to me. I. Do not. Want. Bryce. I can barely even stand to look at him after what he did to me."

"What he did to *you!* Why you hateful, crazy—"

"That's enough!" A middle-aged woman with silver shot auburn hair ranged herself in front of Delaney.

"Aunt Val?" She was early for their lunch date.

"What the hell is going on here?" Miranda

came shoving out of the back, coattails flying. "This is a place of business."

"I've said what I need to say." Gina pointed at Delaney. "You stay the hell away from Bryce."

"You stay the hell away from her," Val said darkly.

With another fulminating glare, Gina stalked out.

Delaney expelled a breath and realized she was shaking.

Val wrapped an arm around her. "Are you okay, honey?"

"I'm fine." She wasn't, but what else was there to say?

"Piper, can you take Mrs. Landon back to two, please. Delaney, why don't you take a minute?" Miranda suggested. Her eyes were kind and sympathetic.

Delaney couldn't bear to look into them. "I don't need a minute."

Val squeezed her shoulders. "Honey, nobody will think any less of you if you—"

Shrugging off her aunt's arm, she headed for

the door to the back. "I need to clean up this mess and get back to work."

Retrieving a broom and dustpan, she dragged the big garbage can from the break room and set to work. Bits of glass were everywhere, and her beautiful flowers lay crushed and mangled. It was a testament to the fact that she'd never escape the worst mistake of her life. And it was probably a premonition of what would ultimately happen to her nascent relationship with Sean. She'd been a fool to think she could ever have a normal life.

Did she like the flowers?

Sean had no idea what time they'd been delivered. He hadn't heard a peep from her all day, and he wondered if they'd been too much too soon. Should he text her or wait for her to contact him? His thumb hovered over the screen of his phone in indecision.

"—if Captain Murphy would care to weigh in?"

Sean jolted at the sarcasm in Ben's voice and realized everybody in the firehouse was looking at him. Hunching his shoulders a little, he shoved the phone into a pocket of his cargo pants. "Sorry, Chief. What were we talking about?"

Ben Rawlings, the newly appointed fire chief—and only full-time, paid employee of the Wishful Volunteer Fire Department—just shook his head. "We're discussing fundraising options to help replace some of our equipment. You're lucky we didn't just nominate you as the cover model for a firefighter's calendar."

Some of the blood drained from Sean's face. "We're not actually doing a calendar, are we?"

"Given the enthusiasm of the Casserole Patrol for the project, we'd probably make bank. But no, at this time, we are not."

Thank God.

Sean's own interaction with the trio of blue-haired ladies had been limited since he'd moved to Wishful last fall, but they had a reputation around town. No well-muscled male under the age of fifty was safe from objectification or covert ass pinching.

Hayden Garrow spoke up. "I heard they're campaigning en masse for a bachelor auction."

Former Navy SEAL Reuben Blanchard shuddered. "God knows what kind of favors they'd expect if they won the bid."

"Lap dances," Dean Coulter suggested.

"Shirtless car washes," Jordan Linley added.

Everybody took a moment of silence out of horror at the thought.

"Actually, that last isn't a bad idea," Sean mused.

"Say what now?" Reuben asked.

"Car washes. It's August and a drought. Everybody's car is dusty. And it's the kind of thing that wouldn't take much advanced planning."

Zeke Hammel lifted one steely brow. "Are you gonna take off *your* shirt in the name of fundraising?"

Yeah, okay, the fifty-something structural engineer wasn't exactly the draw they'd be going for. But Sean knew he was, so he shrugged. "Sure. Women appreciate the kind of bodies we have from this line of work. If they're gonna objectify us anyway, we might as well make some money off it. And at least in this context, it's not some awkward attempt at being sexy. We'd just be washing cars."

"The man has a point," Hayden agreed.

The thirty or so men present for tonight's meeting debated the details—cost, location, traffic flow, and—more importantly, who got nominated for shirtless duty. Other than Ben, Sean was the only member of the department who'd been a professional firefighter before coming on here.

"I'd rather do a pancake breakfast. Everybody likes pancakes," Dewey May proclaimed. The fireplug of a man had already proved himself more than at home in the firehouse kitchen.

"No reason we couldn't do both," Ben said.

Before debate could resume, a chorus of text notifications and pagers went off. Sean yanked out his phone and read the alert.

Structure fire 1489 Edgebrook Dr.

He was moving before he even reached the end of the text, his adrenaline already pumping. This was his first summer in seven years spent somewhere other than on a hotshot crew, fighting side-by-side with other tough-as-nails men and women to contain and defeat forest fires around the country, and he missed it like a limb. While calls to the Wishful Volunteer Fire Department had been pretty regular with the drought, mostly it had been small stuff, readily contained. It wasn't the same as going up against the dragon in all her wild and untamed glory and winning. But after his mom's cancer scare last year, he'd realized he had to give up his career as a hotshot so he could be closer to home, just in case the scare turned out to be real.

The crew moved like a well-oiled machine, their regular drills paying off. In under five minutes, the fire engine rounded the corner onto Edgebrook, with Ben at the wheel. Sean could see the plumes of smoke. The source of the fire was obvious as he leapt off the truck. Flames licked from a garbage can set at the corner of the house. They crawled like a live thing up the side, eating through the siding and rapidly heading for the roof. A woman—the homeowner? —stood in the yard, legs braced, aiming an anemic spray of water from a garden hose at the conflagration. If the wind turned, she was going to get hurt.

"Get her out of the way," Sean ordered.

Hayden hustled over in his turnout gear, while the rest of them hooked up the hose. It wasn't bad. Not yet. But garages tended to be full of flammable materials. They needed to put this out, and fast. Beside the house, Hayden was arguing with the woman, finally just yanking the hose from her hand and dragging her bodily back from the blaze. Once they got real water pumping, the fire was out in minutes.

The damage was minimal, which was rarely

the case. The shingles at the edge of the roof were the only genuine loss, along with the outer wall of the garage. This woman had been extremely lucky. Sean strode over in time to hear Ben begin his questioning.

"—any idea what might have started the fire?"

"I know exactly who started the fire. This has that woman written all over it."

"What woman, Miss Draper?" Ben asked.

"Delaney Newell," she spat.

Sean's step hitched. "That's quite the accusation."

"It isn't the first fire she's set here."

No. There had to be some mistake. Delaney wouldn't do this.

But Miss Draper was still talking. "She got out of the last one, claiming it was an accident, but we knew better. I'm gonna make sure she doesn't get out of this one. I'm pressing charges for arson. Our whole house could've burned down!"

"Let's not get ahead of ourselves," Ben cautioned. "We have to wait on the fire marshal to make a ruling on the true cause of the fire before we can get the law involved."

"Well, when can he come? I want this to be dealt with as fast as possible, before that little bitch weasels out of it."

Sean stepped away, moving to help Hayden and Dean re-roll and stow the hose. They needed to finish up here so they could get back to the firehouse. Whatever the hell was going on, Sean knew he had to get to Delaney first.

CHAPTER 3

A tension headache clawed at the base of Delaney's skull. She ignored it, making another notation in her spreadsheet. What did a headache matter when the rest of her life prospectively hung in the balance?

She'd completed her EMT certification to prove to herself and everyone else that she could finish something important. That she could still make something of herself. She'd loved the training, and she was good at the work, but EMT positions in Wishful were few. Miranda would keep her on at the clinic until something opened up, but who knew when that might be. And she was seriously tempted to keep going and become a paramedic. It was considerably more training, more experience, and would prospectively open up more job options long term. But that was another two years of school, and it wasn't a program offered by Wachoxee County Community College. Which meant that for either option, she'd probably have to leave Wishful.

Delaney glanced over at the one lily that had mostly survived Gina's wrath. Maybe leaving was the best thing. Going somewhere nobody knew her and starting over entirely. Getting away from all her poor decisions. Miranda would give her a good recommendation. She could maybe find some kind of job in the medical field while she went back to school. Something where she could earn enough to pay for a little studio apartment and her tuition without having to resort to student loans. Maybe.

But there was Sean.

It was foolish to include him in the equation. Things between them were hardly advanced enough to justify it. And after today, it was only a matter of time before her past reared up and ruined everything, anyway. Maybe she should leave while she was ahead. Before he looked at her with suspicion. Or worse, like she was crazy.

And yet. Reaching out, she stroked a finger gently down one petal. Her stupid, romantic heart wanted to give things a real try.

A knock sounded on her apartment door, and Delaney jolted. A glance at the clock told her it was nearly ten. Late for somebody to be dropping by. Grateful she hadn't yet changed into the oversized T-shirt she slept in, she headed for the door.

"Sean." Her heart gave a quick bump of excitement as she took him in, standing on her front stoop, his hair still damp from a shower. "Come in." As he moved past her, she caught a faint whiff of smoke. "Did you just finish up a call?"

He scrubbed a hand over his stubbled face.

"Yeah. I just came from a fire at Gina Draper's house."

A brick dropped into Delaney's gut, and whatever hope she'd harbored that they stood a chance died a swift death. He knew. Probably not everything and probably not much of the actual truth, but something anyway. She'd hoped she'd have more time, that she'd get the chance to explain things herself before someone else had the chance to bias him with the embellished version that most people in town liked to tell. But she should've known karma would bite her in the ass yet again. She didn't deserve good things after what she'd done, no matter how much she'd turned her life around since then.

Sean stood there, expression serious, obviously waiting for some kind of reaction from her.

Delaney shut the door, struggling to stay calm. "What happened? Is she okay?"

"She's fine. The fire marshal still has to determine the actual cause, but by all appearances, it started in the outside garbage can and spread up the wall of the garage. You want to tell me why she's accusing you of arson? Why she claims it's not the first fire you've set there?"

So maybe he didn't know yet. Delaney didn't want to tell him. She didn't want to change how he looked at her. But what was the alternative? Letting everybody else in town fill in the gossip version of events? She would have this one chance to tell her side before everybody else got to him. He'd either believe her or he wouldn't. But there was no escaping now.

"Because two years ago, I did start a fire at their house. Not on purpose," she hastened to add. "Not that they believed me then. Which explains why she's so fast to cast aspersions now."

His look of utter disbelief made her feel an iota better. "I think you better start at the beginning."

He wasn't running immediately. Delaney knew better than to think that meant anything more than that Sean was a good guy, who would at least want to hear the entire story before deciding. She gestured him to the sofa, then curled up at the opposite end, arms wrapped around her knees. Because she couldn't stand to watch his face, she stared at a small hole in the knee of her yoga pants.

"That guy you rescued me from at The Mudcat last week is Bryce Kelso. My ex. A little over two years ago, I found out he was cheating on me with Gina. When he left me for her, I... didn't take it well." Understatement of the century. "They hurt me, and I wanted to make them pay. I made a lot of stupid, impulsive decisions. Vandalized his SUV, harassed her, and ultimately left a very graphic message regarding my opinion of his manhood painted in oil-based stain on his prized deck. I nearly got caught at that and ended up shoving the rags under the porch while I made my escape. That's where the fire came in."

"They spontaneously combusted," he guessed.

"Yes. I was hiding out nearby because I

wanted to see the look on Bryce's face when he saw his deck. When I saw the smoke, I called to report the fire myself, but by the time the fire department got there, most of the deck was a loss. I got arrested."

"Jesus, Delaney."

She winced, hating how all of this made her look. "It wasn't my finest moment. But in the end, it was the best thing that could've happened because it got me the help I needed." Because it was the truth, she lifted her head and dared to look at him.

His brows drew together. "Help for what?"

She didn't want to tell him this either, but better he hear the truth from her rather than whatever bastardized version was still floating around town. Not that it would matter. He'd walk away from her after this, and she wouldn't blame him.

But before she could hammer the last nail in the coffin of their fledgling relationship, there was another knock on the door. With a sense of foreboding hanging over her like a shroud, De-

laney went to answer. She was wholly unsur-
prised to find the chief of police standing on
her doorstep.

With a sigh, she stepped back. "You might as
well come in so we can get this over with."

As Chief Greer stepped into Delaney's
apartment, Sean shot to his feet, every instinct
on alert. There wouldn't have been time for the
fire marshal to come out yet and process the
scene. It wouldn't be cool enough for a while
yet. What was he doing here?

Delaney's shoulders were tense and bowed
with resignation, as if this whole process was
familiar. And hell, given what she'd just told
him, maybe it was. But it didn't stop his desire
to shield her from whatever was coming.

Ethan caught sight of him and nodded. "I'm
interrupting. Sorry about that. I need to ask
you some questions." This last he directed at

Delaney. He seemed legitimately apologetic about it.

She crossed her arms over her middle in a gesture of self-protection rather than belligerence. "I expect you do. I'll save some time. I've been here since I got off work at six, alone, until Sean showed up about fifteen minutes ago. No one can corroborate that."

"You've heard about the fire then."

"Sean told me. I'm guessing the fire marshal found signs of arson."

"Actually, he hasn't even been to the scene yet."

Delaney frowned at that.

"Then what are you doing here?" Sean demanded, crossing over to stand beside her, close but not touching. Her posture didn't invite contact.

Unruffled, Ethan only lifted a brow. "Some preemptive groundwork. Gina Draper's already making noises about wanting to press charges, which, obviously, she can't do unless or until Charlie says there's something to charge, but with the history between you two, I have to ask."

A muscle jumped in Delaney's jaw, and her fingers whitened around her elbows. "I know you do. But I didn't do this."

"I understand there was an incident with her at the clinic today."

"What incident?" Sean asked.

She pressed her lips together, closing her eyes and sucking in a breath as if she needed fortification before answering. "Someone saw Bryce talking to me at The Mudcat Friday night and evidently reported back to Gina. She got it into her head that I was trying to steal him back. She came into the clinic, totally irate, smashed the vase of flowers you sent me —they were beautiful, by the way. Thank you. She thought they were from Bryce. Anyway, she threatened me if I didn't stay away from him." Blowing out a breath, she met Ethan's gaze. "I expect she's going to say I had some kind of break because of it and retaliated like this. But I didn't. I've been sticking to my medication. Ask Miranda. She's been monitoring me."

"Medication for what?" Probably it wasn't any of Sean's business, but he hated he knew so little of what was going on. For all he'd spent months as her friend, he felt very on the outside right now, and he didn't like it.

Delaney closed her eyes briefly before lifting them to his. "I'm bipolar. Have been all my life, but it wasn't until they sentenced me to inpatient evaluation and treatment that someone actually diagnosed me. I was put on the proper medication, and I've been fine ever since. I've been fighting tooth and nail to overcome the things I did before that, to get my life together. Reputations in small towns, once earned, are incredibly hard to destroy. Why would I risk all the progress I've made by harassing Gina Draper again over a guy who means nothing to me?"

"You wouldn't." She seemed surprised by the conviction in his voice. "I saw you with Bryce Friday. You wanted nothing to do with him. By the time I got there, you looked like you were about to crawl out of your skin just having to stand within three feet of him at the bar." At the memory of it, Sean wanted to kick the guy's ass all over again. He shifted his attention to Ethan. "She wasn't flirting with him. He was coming on to her and not taking the hint to back the hell off. It sounds to me like Gina's got her own jealous streak going. Doesn't seem outside the realm of possibility that she set the fire herself, trying to make Delaney look bad and cause her trouble as revenge because Bryce seems to be following pattern and straying again. Or at least showing the inclination to stray."

Delaney sucked in a breath. "She hates me enough. But I have a hard time imagining her risking a fire getting out of control in the name of… whatever this is."

"It's a theory," Ethan agreed. "One we'll check out. We'll see what Charlie finds and go from there. I'll get out of your hair. I know you've got an early day tomorrow. Thanks for your time."

"Of course." Delaney walked Ethan to the door. After he'd gone, she wouldn't quite meet Sean's eyes. "I appreciate you coming to talk to me about this. And I wanted to say I've really enjoyed our time together."

What the hell? "What are you talking about?"

"I'm just saying I value our friendship, and I get that you need to walk away."

She expected him to bail on her. The realization had his temper, already close to the surface in the wake of the accusations being flung at her, spiking to dangerous levels.

Beyond insulted and sick with the knowledge that she wouldn't expect this if it hadn't happened to her before, Sean had to fight to keep his voice level. "Is that really what you think of me?"

Something in his tone had her lifting her head. "What?"

"You think I'm going to listen to the ravings of some jealous, bitchy woman and just leave you high and dry."

"No. I just—"

"Because that's just damned insulting. To you and to me."

"But I—" She shook her head. "With the criminal record and the bipolar disorder, I thought—I wouldn't blame you if you didn't believe me."

Her shoulders curled, as if in defense of a blow, and he wanted to beat the shit out of whoever had made her expect this from people. Instead, he closed the distance between them, keeping his hands light as he took hold of her shoulders.

"Of course, I believe you."

She stared up at him in bewildered shock. "Why?"

Gently, because she looked so fragile that one wrong move might break her, he tucked a lock of hair behind her ear, lightly skimming his knuckles over her cheek. "Because the woman I know wouldn't have done any of this."

Her shock shifted to something else akin to awe and gratitude, as if he were a unicorn offering to grant her greatest wish. That something so simple as support and belief in her innocence inspired such a response hit him somewhere low in the gut.

Had he thought her fragile? She'd never have survived everything she must've been through if she'd been anything weaker than steel. But even steel could become brittle after a while.

"I'm not going anywhere." He tipped her face up, and as he pressed a soft kiss to her lips, he made her a promise. "You're not going down for this."

CHAPTER 4

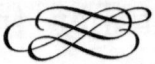

*D*elaney popped a piece of strawberry danish into her mouth and gave a little groan of happiness. "Okay, this was a good idea. Thanks for inviting me to breakfast, Aunt Val."

Val forked up a bite of ooey gooey cinnamon roll. "I figured you could use a little indulgence after that.. unpleasantness yesterday. And I know you hate it, but it's good for you to be seen in public. You've got nothing to hide."

That was true enough, but it went against Delaney's instincts. At the first hint of scandal, she wanted to disappear. She wondered if she'd ever be known as anything other than "that girl who went crazy on her ex and his woman on the side."

"—saw the smoke from my house last night."

At the sound of the voice from a few tables away, Delaney tensed.

"Do they know what caused it?"

"Gina said it was arson."

"Arson! Who would do something like that?"

"She said Bryce's ex is at it again. You remember when all that went down a few years ago. She set their deck on fire."

Delaney hunched further into the booth. Would anybody notice if she just hid under the table?

Val reached out to lay a hand over hers. "Ignore them. You did nothing wrong."

"Since when does that matter in this town?" The weight of powerlessness threatened to crash over her like a tidal wave. She would never overcome this, never get away from it because somebody, somewhere, would always remember and stir it back up.

Her aunt frowned, brows knit together in concern. "People are going to believe what they're going to believe. The important ones know the truth."

That was worth something. Her coworkers would stand by her. And Val. And by some miracle, so would Sean. But not everyone important would side with her.

If her parents got wind of this, they'd probably be first on the bandwagon to ship her back to inpatient treatment. Where they thought she should stay. Far, far away from them. They hadn't supported her two years ago, and in the face of her diagnosis, they'd essentially disowned her. As if she were personally responsible for her screwed up brain chemistry and had brought it on herself. If not for Val's kindness in giving her a home once she got out of the hospital, Delaney didn't know what she would've done.

She turned her hand up and curled her fingers around Val's. "Thank you for always standing by me."

"You know I always will."

She would. No one was as fiercely loyal as Val, who'd faced being the black sheep of the family long before Delaney had earned the title.

Because Val would worry otherwise and start to hover, Delaney put on a happy face and forced herself to choke down the last of her pastry and coffee. "I need to get on to work. Thanks for breakfast."

"You're welcome, honey. And just be a duck about the rest of this. Let it all roll off your back."

Easier said than done, but she offered up a smile and a hug before she hurried out of The Daily Grind, head down, eyes averted.

As soon as she hit the sidewalk, she felt her hard-won control slipping again. Recognizing the beginning of a spiral, she opted to walk for a bit and crossed the street to the town green. Slowing down the breath that had gotten too short and shallow, she worked on letting go of all the voices of recrimination echoing through her head. Finding herself standing in front of the historic fountain, Delaney stopped and sat on the edge. Trailing her fingers through the water, she felt some of the tension ebb.

This wasn't like before. This time she hadn't done anything. There was no evidence to indicate that she had. Even if someone had deliberately caused the fire, she knew it wasn't her. Ethan Greer was a good cop. He'd find out who actually did it, and then the talk would fade again. She'd survived worse. She'd survive this. Somehow.

Digging in her purse, she unearthed a penny. Clutching it in her fist, she focused with all her might on her one wish.

I wish I could finally overcome my past and have a real chance at a new life.

She dropped the coin into the water.

"Morning."

Delaney looked up, and there was Sean, as if she'd summoned him with her wish. And maybe she had because he was smiling down at her like he was genuinely glad to see her. How could he have found out all that stuff last night and not look at her any differently?

The smile she gave him was a lot closer to the real thing. "Morning. I thought you were supposed to be out in the field today." He was dressed in his forestry commission uniform of dark green pants and a khaki shirt.

"I will be shortly. But Eli's in the doghouse with Jessie. Since he's making a Monday morning, forgive-me-for-being-an-idiot gesture over at the pharmacy, I went by the diner to pick up some biscuits to go." He held up a grease-spotted paper bag. "I saw you over here and thought I'd come say hi."

She felt her smile get bigger and couldn't seem to dial it down. "Hi. It's nice to see a friendly face."

He sobered. "Somebody been giving you trouble?"

That instant readiness to defend her was sexy as hell. Delaney was terrified she'd get used to it. Twitching her shoulders in a shrug, she just shook her head. "Not really. People are just talking about the fire."

"That makes you uneasy."

"People in general make me uneasy." It wasn't a lie, even if it wasn't the absolute truth.

She knew he knew it was more than that, but she didn't want to get into it right now. He was a bright spot to her morning, and she wanted to focus on that instead.

"Aren't you due at work here in a bit?" he asked.

"Yeah. I was just breathing in a little nature before I went."

"Walk you to your car?" Sean held out his free hand.

"Why thank you, kind sir." She laid her hand in his and let him tug her up.

Momentum carried her straight into his arms, and she didn't fight it. His arms wrapped around her, pulling her flush against the hard muscles of the body his profession had honed. He was strong and capable, and right here, right now, it felt like he could actually protect her from all the slings and arrows people might hurl at her, be her shelter from the storm. Because that was more than a little appealing, Delaney snuggled into him, tucking her head against his shoulder.

His lips brushed her temple. "You seemed like you could use a hug."

"I definitely can. And you give really great ones."

Because he did, Delaney made no effort to move away, too much enjoying being wrapped quietly in each other by the fountain, as a soft breeze blew, and the birds happily chirped their morning concert.

"I *told* you something was going on between those two!"

Startled, Delaney looked over to see Miss Betty Monroe, Miranda's very nosy neighbor and one third of Wishful's most notorious busybodies, the Casserole Patrol. Her arm was looped companionably through that of Maudie Bell Ramsey, one of her usual partners in crime.

Miss Maudie Bell grumbled. "I thought for

sure it would take another month. That means I lost the pool."

"Pool?" Sean asked.

"Well, of course," Miss Betty explained. "Didn't you know there's a pool up at Dinner Belles about everybody's love life?"

Struggling not to laugh at his poleaxed expression, Delaney started to step back, but he only tightened his hold

Miss Betty beamed. "Good for you for finally going for it, young man! I heard about that kiss at The Mudcat. It's about time." As they made their way past, she leaned closer and whispered conspiratorially, "You should absolutely give her another one of those for the road. Guaranteed to get a girl's day off to the right start!"

"I'll, uh, take that under advisement."

She patted his arm. "You do that. Bye now!"

He held on until they'd disappeared into the diner. "There's a pool?"

Feeling far more cheerful, Delaney eased back. "There's always a pool. How have you lived here this long and not known that? Although I admit, I didn't know there was one on us."

"I really don't know how to feel about that."

She shrugged. "Small towns are all about the gossip. I'd way rather be talked about for being seen with one of the hottest guys in town than for... other things."

Sean's gaze darkened. "Then let's give them something to talk about."

He pulled her in again, laying his lips over hers in a kiss that burned away every thought but the feel of his hands in her hair and the need to get closer.

By the time he stepped back, whatever steadiness she'd found was absolutely lost. A little wobbly on her knees, she stared up at him in a breathless daze. "Thanks."

He grinned. "Anytime."

His hand stayed threaded companionably with hers as they headed to her car, effectively announcing to the world—or this little piece of it—that they were a Thing. The idea of it made her giddy.

"What are you doing tonight?"

Fantasizing about you. "I don't know. I hadn't gotten that far."

"Let me cook you dinner."

She went brows up. "You cook?"

"You'd be hard pressed to find a firefighter who doesn't."

"I don't think a guy has ever cooked for me before."

"Then let me be the first. I'll come by your place around seven?"

"Sure. Do I need to pick anything up?"

"Nah. I'll bring everything I need."

"Then I guess it's a date."

He grinned. "It's definitely a date."

SEAN PULLED up at Delaney's garage apartment about five minutes past seven. He'd needed to drive around the block a few more times to get a handle on his temper after hearing the latest gossip at McSweeny's Market. People were tossing around Delaney's name like her life was the latest "it" show to watch. No wonder she tried so hard to be invisible. He'd wanted to set them straight but recognized that would only fuel the fire. So, by the time he'd checked out, he'd ground down a layer of teeth instead.

Hauling his bags of groceries and supplies up the stairs, he knocked.

From inside she called out, "It's open."

Banishing the last of his irritation with the world, Sean put on a smile and stepped inside. "Hope you're hungry."

Delaney's face lit up at the sight of him, and damn if that didn't make his day. "Hey."

"Well, are you going to introduce us?"

That was when Sean realized they weren't alone. An older woman sat at the little dinette table. He could see a bit of a resemblance, but this woman's red hair tended more toward auburn and was shot through with a few strands of silver, and her lips were thinner.

Though maybe that was because of the suspicion clouding her face as she gave him a once over.

"Sean, this is my aunt, Valerie Gibbons. She lives in the house next door. Aunt Val, this is Sean Murphy."

"The one from the bar?"

Delaney's cheeks pinked, but she didn't lose her smile. "Yes, that one."

Sean put the groceries on the short stretch of counter and turned to offer his hand. "Nice to meet you, ma'am."

After another long survey, Val took it and shook. Sean couldn't be annoyed at the distrust. Val was clearly protective of her niece. He appreciated that there was someone else looking out for her.

"I understand you're fairly new in town."

"Yes, ma'am. I moved to Wishful back in November."

"And you're a firefighter?"

"Just volunteer now. But I was a hotshot for seven years before coming back to Mississippi."

"A what now?"

Sean smiled. "Hotshots are firefighters specifically trained to handle wildland fires. So I spent a lot of time in Idaho and Montana. The name comes from the fact that our crews are sent to handle the hottest parts of the fire."

"They're the most elite firefighters in the country," Delaney added. The pride in her voice made Sean want to hug her.

"Goodness. And now you're here?"

"Now I'm here."

"Do you miss it?" Val asked.

She couldn't know what a loaded question that was. "Like a limb." No point in lying. Delaney knew how he felt about his old job. "But it's more important that I'm close to family."

"Sean's from Lawley," Delaney explained.

"What do you do now?"

This was starting to feel like a job interview. "I'm with the Mississippi Forestry Commission."

"And still fighting fires on the side?"

"Yes, ma'am."

"He's using all his experience to make recommendations to the Commission about wildfire prevention."

"Not that they're doing much listening, but
yeah. Mostly, I've been handling residential
fires with the volunteer fire department here in
Wishful. I was part of the team who responded
to the fire at Gina Draper's place."

Val's face darkened. "Is there any word on
the actual cause of the fire at that harpy's
house?"

Obviously, no love lost there. Sean crossed
his arms to keep from giving in to the urge to
pull Delaney into them. He didn't know how
she'd feel about PDA in front of family. "The
fire marshal said the origin was most likely a
cigarette butt."

"Gina smokes," Delaney announced. "Or she
did, anyway."

"She does," Sean confirmed. "But she's still
swearing left, right, and upside-down she didn't
do it."

Val snorted. "Did the fire marshal rule it arson?"

"Much to Gina's dismay, no. He ruled it probable negligence."

Even from six feet away, Sean could feel the tension leak out of Delaney at that news. She wouldn't be getting another visit from the police.

"Thank God." She closed the distance between them, and he automatically folded her in as she hugged him. "And thank you for not doubting me." She still had that look of wonder, as if she couldn't believe her good fortune.

Sean skimmed his thumb across her cheek. "There was nothing to doubt."

He didn't miss the long, speculative look from her aunt as Delaney laid her head against his shoulder.

Val pushed back from the table. "Well, I'm going to get out of here so you young people can get on with your date. Y'all have a nice dinner. Dee, you let me know if you need anything."

"Thanks, Aunt Val. I'll see you later."

Once the door shut behind her, Delaney laced her hands at the small of his back. "So, what are we having?"

"A firehouse favorite. Homemade mac and cheese with bacon and mushrooms."

"Yum! I sincerely hope that ability to cook is not on your list of requirements for the women you go out with because it's not my strong suit."

"I can teach you."

Her blue eyes sparked. "I'll take you up on that. What can I do to help?"

Sean unloaded the groceries and set her to work grating the assorted cheeses, while he got the pasta water going and started the bechamel sauce. He took advantage of his role as instructor to get up close and personal, demonstrating various techniques. The kitchenette was tiny, but he didn't mind a bit. It meant they kept brushing up against each other. A lingering touch here, a lean in there. By the time the pasta was assembled and poured into a casserole dish to bake, his skin was fairly humming. As soon as he slid it into the oven and set a timer, Delaney hauled him in and fastened her mouth to his.

The hungry, possessive kiss stirred his blood. Sean wasn't used to boldness from her, but he was all kinds of on board with this flash of fire. Boosting her up until she wrapped her legs around his waist, he carried her to the sofa. With the two neurons still firing in his brain, he pulled up short, turning to sink down with her in his lap rather than laying her out beneath him. This way she could set the pace and keep control. Even if it killed him.

Her silky hair was down and loose around her shoulders. Sean buried his hands in it as she devoured his mouth like she needed him to breathe. Jesus, that was a turn on. It drained the last of the blood from his brain straight into his crotch. Delaney, observant woman that she was, took total advantage of that fact, shifting until she rubbed her core against the bulge behind his fly.

"Jesus God," he groaned.

She stilled. "I'm sorry. Should I stop?"

"I might die if you do." He might die if she didn't, but what a way to go.

Her wicked smile was a delightful surprise before she kissed him again, starting to rock in his lap. He dipped a hand under her shirt, skimming it up her bare back. Soft. She was so soft. She pressed closer, and he wrapped an arm around her hips, holding her tighter against his erection. They kissed and kissed and kissed some more until he was all but blind and deaf to anything but her. His control hung by a thread, but he'd promised himself he'd go at her pace.

"Can I touch you?" he asked.

"Please, God, yes."

Murmuring a silent hallelujah, Sean flicked open her bra as she stripped off his shirt. The unmitigated lust in her eyes at the sight of his bare chest was almost enough to snap his restraint. He needed to see her, needed to touch her. He tugged her shirt up and off and took one rosy nipple into his mouth. Her head fell back on a moan. Taking that for approval, he licked and sucked. She rocked faster, her breath coming in delicious gasps. Filling his palm with her other breast, he kneaded the weight of it until he found a rhythm she liked. And when she whimpered, when he couldn't take it anymore, he thrust his hips against her, rocking until her arms tightened around his shoulders and her every muscle shook as the climax ripped through her.

Drowsy and sated, she slumped against him. And it didn't matter that he was on the verge of coming in his pants like a teenager or that he wouldn't be able to walk properly for a while. Because seeing her come apart like that in his arms, his name on her lips, was the best damned experience of his life. It made him feel about twenty feet tall, as if he could be anything and everything she needed.

He kissed her brow. "You're so beautiful."

Delaney tensed and slowly lifted her head, not quite looking him in the eye. "I, um, got carried away."

"Please know that I will happily carry you off like that any time you want." He was already thinking about doing it again, using his hands, his mouth. But that was getting ahead of things. If he got her naked, right now he wouldn't be able to make himself stop. So he wouldn't get her naked yet.

"I... oh... but you..." She glanced down at his crotch.

The timer went off.

Sean kissed her quickly, shifting her off his lap before his little brain overtook good sense and he rolled her beneath him. Patience was a virtue. Right?

"Dessert can wait. Supper's ready."

CHAPTER 5

*D*elaney really wanted dessert. She'd wanted dessert almost every day the past two weeks she and Sean had been sharing dinner together. But while he was all about satisfying *her*, he'd only go so far and no further. Not that she hadn't been enjoying the cooking lessons and the making out and the orgasms. She had no idea what the deal was. He wanted her. She could tell that for certain every time they were together. He seemed to have some old-fashioned sensibility about a certain amount of time needing to pass before they fell into bed. Maybe it was because he was a preacher's kid.

As she sat across from him at the dinette table over a plate of spicy chicken enchiladas, only half-listening to a story about something Eli Hamilton had done at work, a horrifying thought occurred to her. Surely... *surely,* he wasn't planning to wait until marriage or engagement or something?

"Something wrong with the enchiladas?"

Delaney blinked. "What?"

"You made a face. Something wrong?"

I want you to take me to bed.

Yeah, she wasn't quite liberated enough to just blurt that out over a plateful of Mexican food.

"No. Nothing's wrong." To prove it, she smiled and forked up another bite. "My mind was wandering a bit is all. Sorry."

His gray-green eyes searched hers. "Are people giving you trouble over the fire?" The hard set of his jaw said he was prepared to take care of it if they were.

It was still such an alien thing to have someone else ready and willing to defend her.

"Actually, no. Other than Gina, no one's said anything to me directly. The rumor mill seems to have died down faster this time. Or, at least, people are keeping it to themselves when I'm around." Delaney would call that a win.

Sean frowned. "What was it like for you before?"

She set her fork down.

"You don't have to talk about it if you don't want to. I'm just trying to understand where you're coming from."

"No, it's fine. I don't mind talking about it." To buy a few moments, she sipped at her beer to wet her throat. "It was hell. That probably seems overdramatic."

"I've seen how you react to being in public. Nothing seems overdramatic."

He'd seen and hadn't judged her. He had, in fact, done what he could to shield her, rolling with her preference to stay in rather than go out. He couldn't understand how much that meant to her.

"My arrest was highly publicized locally. Everybody was talking about it because I was the girl who snapped. Details got embellished. Plenty of outright lies were told. But the fundamental truth was that I had seriously screwed up, and that made me the juiciest gossip to hit this town in years. My parents were furious and disappointed. When I got sent to inpatient treatment instead of jail, they didn't care. When I got diagnosed and there was suddenly a reason for my erratic, reckless behavior, they didn't care. After my release, I needed help to pick up the pieces of my life. They still didn't care. They walked away."

"What do you mean they walked away?"

"I mean, they disowned me. I've spoken to them once in the last two years. When they see me in public, they go the other way."

The flash of temper was instant, but Sean's voice remained steady. "That's appalling."

Delaney shrugged. She'd accepted where she

stood with her family and decided it was their loss. "It was more fodder for the gossip mill. I'd made my bed, as it were, and people wanted to see me lie in it. Everywhere I went, they stared and whispered. And then there were the people who felt it was their 'Christian duty' to remind me of the error of my wicked ways to my face. I developed a lot of anxiety and sank into a major depression. If not for Aunt Val, I'd have been out on the street. She took me in, gave me a home. And when I lost my job and couldn't find another, she let me take over the computer stuff for her eBay business. And that was good, because it let me keep a low profile. My best defense was to simply hide. If I wasn't visible, people were less likely to remember me and re-hash things all over again."

"Why didn't you just leave?"

Too restless to keep sitting, she cleared her plate and started in on the dishes. "I thought about it. But I had no money, no contacts. I've lived in Wishful my entire life. I didn't know where I could go."

Sean added his plate to the sink and took up his position with the dish towel. "You've obviously turned things around."

Delaney tipped her head in acknowledgment. "Started to. Miranda took a chance on me by giving me a job at the clinic, and that was huge. It forced me back into dealing with the public and getting over some of my anxiety." She offered a small smile. "That's actually what first got me interested in you. You didn't know any of this when you met me, and you just treated me like I was normal."

"You are normal."

"I've got a boatload of people who'd argue that with you." She started to plunge her hands into the soapy water where the casserole dish was soaking, but he grabbed her by the shoulders and turned her to face him.

"You've got a mood disorder. So what? They're common. I've had friends and family who've fought with depression and anxiety. Other hotshots from my crew who struggled with PTSD. Everybody's likely to have something in their lifetime. Hence, you're normal."

Her heart clutched. "Every time you say stuff like that, it makes me breathless."

"Then I'll keep saying it until you believe it."

What had she done to deserve this man? Stepping into him, she framed his face, thinking that maybe, after all this, she really could ask for what she wanted. "Sean, I—"

The knock on the door had her pulling away.

"Are you expecting someone?" Sean asked.

"It's probably Aunt Val. She hasn't stopped by yet to check on me today."

But it wasn't her aunt at the door. Ethan stood on her stoop, another officer right behind.

Delaney went rigid. "Now what?"

"Can we come in?" Ethan asked.

She stepped back, letting Ethan and Rowan Beale enter.

"We need—"

"—to ask me some questions. Yeah, I know the routine. What is it?"

Sean put an arm around her, and she relaxed a fraction.

"Where were you tonight between six and around seven-thirty?"

Delaney eased another notch. "I've been with Sean. We went to McSweeney's at about 5:30 to pick up stuff for dinner and came back here to make enchiladas."

Sean dug into his wallet. "Here's the time-stamped receipt. We left the market at 5:50. I'm sure we're on whatever cameras they've got." He gestured to the pile of dinner dishes. "Proof we made everything tonight and didn't just pull something out of the freezer."

"What exactly are you checking up on me to make sure I didn't do?"

"Somebody tossed a Molotov cocktail into Bryce Kelso's car," Officer Beale reported.

Delaney stared at her. "I'm sorry, what?"

Ethan rocked back on his heels. "It seems while Bryce was playing a pickup game of basketball at the community center, he left his windows down, as people are apt to do down here when it's hotter than the Devil's bathtub. Someone took advantage of that fact and tossed a flaming bottle of kerosene into his backseat."

"Was anybody hurt?" Delaney asked.

"No. And the fire didn't spread beyond his car, thank God," Rowan added.

Sean checked his phone. "Why didn't I get the alert for the fire?"

"Ben was part of the pickup game. He managed to put it out before the call went out," Ethan explained.

"And because it was Bryce Kelso, you automatically have to check up on Delaney." Sean's tone was biting.

Delaney laid a hand on his arm. "It's fine. He's just doing his due diligence."

"It's not fine. It's harassment. And it's going to get people talking again."

"If I don't check and confirm she has an alibi —which you are handily enough around to provide—people will keep talking and spreading lots of variations that aren't the truth. This will quash the rumors quicker," Ethan said easily. "Have you had any other interactions with Bryce or Gina since the fire?"

"No. Miranda has banned them both from the clinic, and I haven't run into them anywhere else in town."

Another brief tap sounded on the door before it swung open, and Aunt Val walked in. "What's going on?"

"Somebody set Bryce's car on fire," Delaney said.

Val's mouth dropped open in shock. "Well, you didn't do it! You've been joined at the hip with that nice boy there for the last two weeks."

"We know," Ethan assured her. "Your niece has an alibi for the time in question. She's not in any kind of trouble."

The glare Val shot him wasn't mollified. "Bryce Kelso is an asshole. It's entirely possible this has everything to do with him and nothing to do with Delaney. There's no reason to keep bothering her."

"We're exploring every avenue," Ethan promised. "Thanks for your time."

As soon as the door shut behind them, Val sniffed in disgust. "I don't know when they're going to stop doing this to you. It's appalling, that's what it is."

"We're in full agreement on that," Sean told her.

"Y'all, Ethan's right. We all know that anything that happens to Gina and Bryce is going to come back to me, so long as I live in this town. By coming straight here to verify my alibi, it'll nip the gossip about me in the bud. I'm innocent. We all know it, and so do the police. With them to back me up, it's going to be fine."

IT WASN'T FINE.

A little over a week after the car fire, the police still hadn't nailed the perpetrator. The general public didn't seem overly concerned with minor details like the truth, so they were falling back on their favorite scapegoat. Delaney shouldn't have been surprised. She knew what people were like. She'd been down this road before. But after all the work she'd put in, she'd thought she'd made actual progress in overcoming her reputation.

When she'd gone for coffee at The Grind and someone accidentally spilled their mochaccino down her shirt, she'd rolled with it. Accidents happened. When Yvonne Woodman at the bank deliberately ignored Delaney to wait on people who'd come in after her, she'd put on a brave face. Yvonne was a friend of Bryce's mama, after all. But when she and Sean had gone out to Los Pantalones for dinner the other night, Delaney had overheard their server asking to switch sections with another server, specifically because of her. It hadn't mattered that Meghan McGrory—a patient from the clinic—had cheerfully stepped into the breach and gotten them a big bowl of queso on the house. There was no clinging to the delusion that she'd made any inroads in the court of public opinion. Despite evidence to the contrary, people still wanted to believe the worst of her.

The weight of Delaney's anxiety mounted with each passing day. Going out in public was getting harder and harder. She was constantly on edge, waiting for the next slight, the next insult. When Sean had called to say he was running late and would she stop by McSweeney's to pick up some Velveeta for the chicken spaghetti he was making for dinner, she'd almost said no and begged off seeing him tonight. Her capacity for pretending everything was fine was stretched to the breaking point. Crying all over him was so not the next relationship level she was interested in. But neither did she want to just be alone with her feelings. That was the start of a dark road she had no intention of traveling again.

Head down, she strode through the automatic doors of the market. As she was only after one thing, she bypassed the shopping carts and headed toward the far aisle, dodging and weaving around other shoppers. At least two people stopped and stared after her.

It doesn't matter. It doesn't matter. She repeated the mantra in her head as she made her way to the tail end of the aisle where the Velveeta was kept. But the shelf was empty, with nothing but a bright yellow sale tag.

Are you kidding me? Did everybody in town decide they needed to make cheese dip tonight?

Unwilling to give up just yet, Delaney circled the store until she found one of the employees. "Do you know if there's any more Velveeta in the back?"

"Everything's out on the floor for the sale. But we had a stack out at the front of the store. There might still be some there."

"Thanks." Delaney retraced her steps, searching for the display she'd missed in her single-minded trek through the first time. There. The familiar yellow brick, the color of boxed mac and cheese sauce, stood out like the lone survivor of a siege.

Zoned-in on her target, Delaney made a

beeline, reaching out for the brick of processed, cheesy goodness. She didn't realize someone else was there until she lifted the box and saw a hand on the other end.

"Oh, I'm sorry." The apology was out before she even looked up to see who the hand belonged to.

Clarice Hopper Morris sneered, as if she smelled something foul, and let go. "No, you take it. I wouldn't want you to think I was taking something that belongs to you."

Delaney's mouth dropped open. She wanted to say something in protest, but it was just like that night at The Mudcat with Bryce. She couldn't seem to make herself respond.

Clarice lifted one tweezed brow. "Cat got your tongue?"

Chest tight, Delaney felt as if the entire tower of canned tomatoes had toppled over on her. The box fell from her fingers and crashed to the floor.

"Still bullying folks, Clarice? I'd have

thought you'd moved on from high school by now."

Clarice rolled her eyes. "Still playing patron saint of outcasts, I see."

A tanned forearm reached between them and picked up the Velveeta. The arm ended in broad shoulders and a scruffy-jawed face bearing an easy expression. "Why don't you just go on about your business, Clarice?"

With another huff, the other woman sashayed down the cereal aisle.

Delaney's rescuer turned her way. "Don't pay her any mind. She's been a bitch on wheels since she was knee high, and she skipped out on her remedial class in how to be a decent human being."

"I... thank you." She picked her jaw up off the floor. The guy looked familiar, but she was so rattled, she couldn't think why.

He offered the box of Velveeta. "I'm just gonna pass this over to you because I have it on good authority that Sean's making his famous chicken spaghetti, and I figure that's awesome enough to make up for the bad taste that whole encounter left in your mouth." When she didn't take it, he angled his head. "You are Delaney, right? Sean Murphy's girlfriend?"

Speak like a normal human. "I... yes. I'm sorry, I can't quite place you."

He grinned. "That'd be because we've never been formally introduced. I'm Ben Rawlings. Sean and I work together at the fire department."

Delaney's brain kicked into gear, and she realized why he looked familiar. He was one of the responding firefighters who'd put out the deck fire at Bryce and Gina's. There was no way he had put two and two together between that girl and the one his friend was dating. He'd never have intervened if he had.

As the silence dragged out, Ben's expression shifted from good humor to one of concern. Any moment now, he'd figure out who she really was. She needed to get out of here before she watched yet one more person look at her like she was something to be scraped off a shoe.

"It's nice to meet you, Ben. I'm sorry, I have to go."

"Wait. Don't forget your cheese. Sean's chicken spaghetti is so good, it could make the angels weep."

Forcing what she hoped looked like a smile instead of a grimace, Delaney took the offered box and muttered thanks, bolting for the register so she could make her escape.

CHAPTER 6

"It might've been nothing, but she seemed upset when she left. I thought you'd want to know," Ben said.

It wasn't nothing any more than the other incidents this week had been nothing, but Sean didn't tell his friend that. "Thanks, man. I appreciate you letting me know."

"No problem. And enjoy that chicken spaghetti!"

He disconnected the call and tossed the phone on the bathroom counter, wishing now he hadn't asked her to stop by the market. He could've gone himself after showering off his day in the field.

No matter how much she'd spent the last week clinging to the idea that everything was fine, Delaney was nearing the end of her rope. Frustration boiled his blood. In the absence of another suspect, people seemed determined to blame her for the car fire. The fact that Sean was her iron-clad alibi didn't seem to matter one whit. Everybody assumed he was lying for her because they were sleeping together. Ironic, considering he hadn't taken her to bed yet. He was an old-fashioned kind of guy, one who believed such things were better if you took the time to develop a legitimate emotional connection with your partner. It's what they'd been doing the past few weeks of sharing meals. But tonight, she needed something more than his chicken spaghetti, and he knew exactly what he needed to do.

Twenty minutes later, he pulled his truck up to her garage apartment. She didn't answer his knock. Riding on instinct, he trotted downstairs and headed to her aunt's house next door. Val answered the door, a mix of concern and irritation written on her face. With him or the situation?

"Is she here?"

Val jerked a thumb over her shoulder. "In the back."

Sean trailed her into the living room. The smell hit him first... a pungent mix of... he didn't know what. The entire room was covered with open boxes and what seemed like hundreds of... what were those? Jar candles? Maybe this was the eBay business Delaney had mentioned.

She sat on the aging sofa, a box of tissues beside her. At least half a dozen crumpled ones were piled on the coffee table. Her eyes were red-rimmed, but at the sight of him, she made an effort to smile. "Hey. Sorry, I got side-tracked and didn't realize what time it was."

"I can see that. Ben called me. Sounds like you had a lousy day."

She winced. "It wasn't all bad, but it wasn't all great either."

The bitch had made her cry. Or really, it was probably a culmination of all the insults and indignities she'd endured this week. Sean wished he could crack the accusers' heads until they saw reason, but that wasn't an option, so he'd settle for doing what he could to make her feel better. "Come here."

He tugged her up, pulling her into his arms. She burrowed in on a sigh, holding him tight and nestling her head against his shoulder. Some of the tension leeched out of her as he held her. He wanted to wrap her up and protect her from the big bad world. She'd had little enough protection in her life, and she deserved that.

Sean pressed a kiss to her brow. "I wish I could stop all this."

Delaney shrugged. "Them's the breaks. You can't control other people. I'll be all right."

"Honey, I know I've been pushing you to get out there and hold your head up high, but I think maybe I was wrong. This has been so hard on you." Val knit her hands. "Maybe, for right now, you should actually listen to your instincts. Cave up for a while until they sort out who's actually harassing Bryce."

"I didn't do anything wrong." Exhaustion underscored the statement. How often had she been forced to repeat that?

"I know you didn't. But people suck, and I'm worried that the strain of all this is going to set you back."

"You're worried it'll trip another manic episode where I do something reckless," Delaney corrected.

Val spread her hands. "You keep saying you're fine, but it's a reality. It could happen. You know how important it is for you to control your stress level. And I wouldn't want to see you lose any more ground because you didn't take proper care of yourself."

Delaney frowned in reluctant consideration. Sean hated it. He hated the idea of her having to backtrack, being forced into hiding because people were idiots. But Val wasn't entirely wrong.

"You do need to blow off some steam. But holing up at home isn't the way to do it. We're not staying in tonight."

She lifted her head with a grimace. "I appreciate the effort to cheer me up, Sean, but I'm really not up for going out. Besides, I've been hearing tales of your chicken spaghetti."

"The chicken spaghetti can wait until we get back."

"Back? From where?"

"We're getting out of town for the weekend."

She blinked. "We're doing what now?"

"We're going camping."

"Camping," she repeated.

"Yeah. Peace and quiet, no technology, no crowds. It's just what you need."

Her brow furrowed. "To be clear, you mean actual camping? Like with tents and sleeping bags and no electricity."

Please don't be one of those can't-stand-to-be-in-

nature women. "Yeah. The truck's all packed. You just need to pack a bag."

"It's August. In Mississippi." Val pointed out.

"It'll be September next week, and I know the perfect place to keep cool." Somewhere they wouldn't run the chance of being interrupted, should things head in the direction he hoped.

"It's already dinner time." There was something underneath Val's patient, arguing-with-a-child tone. She wanted Delaney to stay put, but that was the last thing her niece needed.

"It is, as you've pointed out, August. We've still got another two or three hours of daylight. Plenty of time to get there and set up camp, prep some dinner." Sean laced both his hands with Delaney's. "Come on. Would you rather mope around at home, hiding out from the world and giving them reason to suspect you've got something *to* hide, or would you rather go on out and keep living?" Maybe it was unfair to appeal to her need for progress, but he wasn't above using whatever means at his disposal to give her what she needed.

With a grave expression she said, "That depends."

"On?" If it was something within his control, he'd do it.

The corner of her mouth twitched in the faintest of smiles. "Did you pack the makings for s'mores?"

"I NEVER WOULD HAVE IMAGINED USING peanut butter cups to make s'mores." Delaney took another bite, enjoying the hit of salty and sweet on her tongue.

"You have to agree, it's superior to the usual way. Even if we're having to cook them over a camp stove because of the burn ban."

"It's too hot for a normal fire, anyway. And yes, I agree that this is better. Especially the part where we have them first and save normal dinner for later."

Sean grinned, his mouth streaked with a mix of chocolate and gooey marshmallow. His tongue darted out to catch the trail, and Delaney had to look away. She'd been thinking far too much about other things he could do with it.

"Feeling a little better?" he asked.

She polished off her s'more and leaned back in her camp chair with a contented sigh. "I am. This was a good idea. Even if it is August."

"Temps are dropping now that the sun has gone down. I wager we've got another half hour or so of twilight before it starts to really get dark." He held out the bag of marshmallows. When she waved it off, he closed them up and stowed them back in a pack, then turned off the stove. "Val didn't want you to come."

"She just worries."

"I can't decide if she approves of me or not."

"I think the real issue is that she misses me. I've been spending every spare minute with you, so Aunt Val and I haven't been hanging out as much. It's a change, and she has a hard time with change. We got really close after I got out of treatment, bonding over our mutual status as black sheep of the family. Before that, she'd been on her own for a long time. She was lonely. I worry about how she'd take it if I left."

"Left the apartment next door or left town?"

That was the question, wasn't it? She'd wanted to discuss it with someone, and who better than the guy who'd rapidly become a prominent feature in her life? "I've been thinking about doing paramedic training."

Sean leaned toward her, his face alight. "Yeah? That's great. Why the hesitation? Is it just because you're worried about your aunt?"

"Well, that. But I don't want to leave you either."

"I can get a job anywhere. There's almost always a demand for firefighters."

Delaney hesitated, staring at him. "You'd be willing to go somewhere else for me?"

He didn't bat an eye. "Yeah."

"After just three weeks?" Surely, he'd come to regret such a rash decision if he made it.

"We were friends for months before that," he reminded her. "Don't get me wrong, I like

Wishful. But I'm not from there like you are. I needed a job that would put me closer to my family in Lawley. It happened that the one with the forestry commission meant it made more sense for me to live in Wishful's corner of the county. Which I'm not in any position to regret because it brought me to you. I'm not gonna walk away from what's between us if it means relocating."

Delaney marveled at what she'd done to deserve this amazing man who actually put her first. Was he her karmic payback for all the hell she'd endured while trying to turn her life around? It was a nice thought—the idea that he was her reward for sticking it out and fighting.

"Is this whole selfless streak just how you're wired?"

"Nah. It's totally you."

That he said it with the ease of absolute truth left her with all the warm fuzzies and a bit of a knot in her throat. Had Bryce ever done *anything* to put her first? Their relationship had seemed solid enough while she was in it—up to the moment she'd found out he was cheating on her. But looking back on their two years together, with these weeks with Sean as a yardstick, she could see Bryce fell short in every category. He'd been selfish and unsupportive, and he'd made her believe that was all her fault.

By contrast, Sean's belief in her made her feel strong. Even before they'd been together, he'd been a good friend to her, building her up, cheering her on. When she wasn't feeling strong, he never belittled her. Instead, he made sure she felt safe and protected, like he'd take on the world in her name. It was heady and romantic and still kind of unbelievable. There was no contest here as to who the better man was. And for now, at least, he was hers.

Moved and needing to get back on even footing, Delaney cleared her throat. "Well, the discussion can wait until later. I wouldn't be able to start anywhere before spring semester, anyway." And by then maybe she'd be more confident that they were really solid enough to survive a move together.

"Fair enough. I'll just say one more thing. Val would want the best for you, and she has to be proud of you for getting your life together and on track. I know I sure as hell am. You're freaking amazing for how hard you've worked, how far you've come."

God. Could he possibly understand what that meant to her? Probably not.

Sean changed the subject, as if she wasn't sitting here on the edge of blubbering. "You ready to start on actual dinner?"

Swallowing back emotion, Delaney searched for a little of the easy flirtation. "I'm still too hot to eat much. You did promise you knew where to cool off."

"So I did." He shoved out of his chair and offered his hand. "C'mon."

Delaney curled her fingers in his, reveling in the solid feel of them. How could so small a gesture make her feel so grounded?

"Do we need to take a flashlight?"

"Won't need it. It's a full moon tonight, and I know where we're going." He grabbed a blanket and a couple of towels and led her several dozen yards away to a skinny little creek.

Delaney eyed it. "Um...it's a little small." Were they going to splash around in it like kids?

Sean snorted. "It does the trick when you need it to. But no, this isn't it. It's just the handy trail to where we're going."

She followed him along the creek bank for several more minutes as the last of the sun faded. It was already cooler beneath the canopy of trees. The creek ended in a pond about fifty feet across. A thick fringe of greenery surrounded most of it in a natural wall, with a break in the branches above revealing a swatch of night sky.

"Oh, that's more like it. But we left our swimsuits back at camp."

"We can go back if you really want, but I didn't figure we needed them." As punctuation to the statement, Sean stripped off his t-shirt, exposing the chiseled plane of his abs and chest.

Delaney's mouth went dry. She dragged her

gaze back up to his face to find him watching her.

"Totally your call."

She understood that this wasn't just a matter of skinny dipping. This would be the first time they'd been fully naked together, and neither of them was under any delusion about where that would lead.

She sent up a fervent prayer of thanks.

Finally.

Anticipation beating thick in her blood, Delaney began to strip.

DELANEY'S HANDS went to the button of her shorts, and all the blood in Sean's head promptly drained south. With a sexy smile, she shimmied out of them, revealing bikini cut underwear in a blue that probably matched her eyes. For a few seconds, he forgot how to work a zipper. Crossing her arms, she tugged her shirt up and off. The bra had matching polka dots. Sean never knew polka dots could be sexy. Though he was reasonably sure Delaney would be sexy in a potato sack.

"Is the plan to swim or just watch?" she asked.

Words, Murphy. Use them. "A man who doesn't stop to appreciate a view like that isn't any kind of man at all."

With a quirk of her lips, she glanced down at the erection tenting his shorts. "I don't think there's any question where you fall on that scale."

"I feel like this is a semi-permanent state around you."

She reached a hand to her back and unhooked her bra, drawing it down her arms and adding it to the pile of clothing at her feet. Her nipples already stood at attention, and Sean wanted his mouth on them. "Well, then, I promise to make it all better." She turned her back to him as she nudged the panties down and stepped out of them. Casting a wicked grin over her shoulder, she stepped toward the bank. "You just have to come get me."

Sean watched, transfixed, as she walked naked into the pond like some kind of wild nature goddess. What exactly had he been waiting for? He couldn't remember as he stripped out of the last of his clothes at lightning speed, pausing only to pull the strip of condoms from his pocket and place them within easy reach of the quick pallet he made of the blanket. Then he dove in after her, slicing cleanly through the water. She shrieked with laughter as he hooked her around the waist and pulled her back to his chest.

"Gotcha."

She wriggled in his grasp until his erection nestled against the curve of her ass. "Not yet, you don't."

Sean nearly swallowed his tongue. "This won't last very long if you keep that up."

Delaney laid her head back on his shoulder, skimming her lips over his jaw. "I figure the last three weeks have been foreplay. I'm completely good with fast. Then slow. Then fast again. Basically, any way I can get you, for as long as humanly possible."

Sean tightened his hold on her to keep her from turning to face him. "You're going to kill me."

With an unapologetic shrug she said, "It's been a long time for me, and I've been thinking about this, with you, for months."

"So have I. All the more reason to slow things down and make it memorable." Easier said than done as the effort of kicking to keep them afloat was creating a delicious friction between her very naked body and his. Inches. Just bare inches and he could be buried inside her.

She reached back and sifted her fingers through the hair at his nape. "Then what exactly have you been waiting for?"

"I didn't want to rush you." It had seemed like the honorable thing to do.

Her lips twitched. "Sean, I appreciate that you want to take care of and protect me, but have I given you any sign at any point during the multiple orgasms over the past few weeks that I am not completely on board with this?" To punctuate the question, she rolled her hips, stroking his cock through her folds.

"No." But the word came out as a strangled sound in the back of his throat as he instinctively clamped an arm around her hips, holding her tighter against his length.

Delaney undulated again. "You've spent the last month—longer—doing everything you can to be exactly what I need. Right now, I just need you. All of you. Inside me."

It took every shred of control he had not to just take her right there, right then. Instead, he bent and nipped lightly at her shoulder. "You're going to have to have a little patience."

"I'm not great with patience."

"I'll make sure you're properly rewarded."

Sean shifted his grip, cupping one breast in his big palm as he slid the other hand down her belly, between her legs. He loved how she opened for him. He slid his fingers along her sex, exploring, arousing.

Delaney dropped her head back against his shoulder on a hissed breath. "God, I love it when you touch me."

He found her clit and circled it, and she bucked against his hand. "I love how responsive you are."

"I need more."

Sean eased one finger inside her, relishing her ragged breathing and the flexing of her body around him. Tonight, tonight, that would finally be the rest of him. But not just yet. When she whimpered, he added a second finger to the first and began to drive her up, ruthless, relentless, until she shattered on a scream under the first evening stars.

Fierce satisfaction swelled in Sean's chest as Delaney went limp in his arms. All traces of the stress and strain of the week vanished. "Now I've got you where I want you."

"Pretty sure you don't as we're in here and the condoms are way over there."

He chuckled. "Relaxed. I've got you relaxed. The rest is coming."

"I hope that means you finally will be. Much as I've enjoyed your ministrations, this has all felt very one-sided."

"I want you. And tonight, I have every intention of having you. Several times." With that in mind, he towed her back toward the bank.

"Thank God."

As soon as his feet hit bottom, he scooped Delaney up against his chest and carried her out of the water. They'd soak the blanket, and he couldn't even care. He wanted this, wanted her too much.

Gently, he laid her down, then bent to check for the condoms. When he turned back, one in his hand, she was stretched out, fair skin all but glowing in the moonlight, hair slicked back like a selkie.

"Christ, you're beautiful."

Her lips curved in a secret smile, and she parted her legs, reaching for him. Sean rolled on the condom and knelt, skimming his hands up her thighs. He shook his head. "Not like this."

The smile faded. "I swear to God—"

Before she could complete the thought, he'd rolled, reversing their positions.

"The ground's hard, even with the grass, and I've got a good sixty pounds on you. You be on top."

"I can work with that." She shimmied down his body until their hips aligned and ran her hands up and over his chest. "You have the most gorgeous body. I really want to explore all of it. With my tongue."

Sean went impossibly harder. "I tortured you. Turnabout seems like fair play here."

Delaney grinned. "Oh, it will be. But next time. Right now, I need you." So saying, she reached between them and guided him to her entrance, sinking down a scant inch.

Muscles quivering, Sean forced himself to hold still, to let her control this. As she'd said, it had been a long time, and she was tight. Bending low, she captured his mouth in delicious, lingering sips as she continued the slow rise and fall on his cock, taking him deeper with each roll of her hips. His world narrowed down to the glorious, wet grip of her body around his. When he was buried to the hilt, she bowed back with a moan of pleasure that matched his own.

Her eyes found his, suddenly fierce. "I want this. I want you."

She took his mouth again and began to move. Sean met her kiss for hungry kiss, tongue tangling with hers. He forgot they were outside, forgot it was the dead of summer, forgot any kind of finesse. He forgot everything but Delaney and the heat they made between them. When the fire turned, it drove itself and them to greater frenzy. And when he knew all hope was lost, when the blaze couldn't be controlled, he reached between them to send her over the edge. Then he surrendered to the flame.

CHAPTER 7

*L*ate Sunday afternoon, Delaney climbed the steps to her apartment and wondered if she was walking funny. Her body felt deliciously sore and used in all the best possible ways. She should've been exhausted. They'd barely slept. Instead, she was deliriously happy, maybe for the first time in her life.

Sean dumped her bag just inside her doorway but stayed on the stoop.

"Aren't you coming in?"

He shook his head and drew her out to

stand with him. "We both know what will happen if I come in, and I have somewhere to be in half an hour."

Grinning, Delaney looped her arms around his shoulders. "You're an efficient man. I'm sure we could do all sorts of interesting things in half that time."

"Vixen," he growled, nipping at her lips. "I'm not coming in."

Only half feigning disappointment, she sighed. "Okay, fine. You have to go be all responsible. But thank you for an amazing weekend. It was just what I needed."

"I was happy to come to your rescue, milady."

"My hero."

"Always." Releasing her, he stepped back and kissed her hand. "I'm going now before I give in to temptation."

He was already at the base of the steps before she could draw a full breath. "Be safe if you get called out tonight."

"Absolutely. I'll call you later." With another

quick wave, he was in his truck and pulling out of the drive.

Floating on a cloud of well-sated bliss, Delaney headed for the shower. Camping had been an excellent idea to get out of town and have all the privacy they could want, but there was simply no substitute for hot, running water. She gloried in the beat of the spray on her muscles and the sensation of the faint layer of sweat washing away. As she poured shampoo into her palm, she caught herself humming.

Well, and why shouldn't she? She was in lust and very serious like with an amazing, thoughtful guy, who was in lust and very serious like right back. That hero complex of his was crazy hot, not because she had a rescue fantasy—although she might be developing one—but because in a dozen small ways, he was constantly proving that he paid attention and he cared about her. And he used that knowledge to take care of her in a way that didn't make her feel incapable or stifled, just supported.

Delaney paused, fingers tangled in the soapy mass of her hair.

That was the feeling she hadn't been able to identify the past few months. She felt stifled in this place. But it wasn't just the tiny studio apartment. It was the entire routine, the life she'd been living with her aunt for the past couple of years. Like the camping, it had been exactly what she'd needed when she got out of treatment, but she'd grown to need something else. She was afraid to admit that she'd grown to need some*one* else because things with Sean were still so new. But the fact of it was hanging out there, whether she admitted it or not.

She was at a turning point. She could stay with the familiar, the safe, continuing to plod along in the life that had become—other than Sean—something of a rut. Or she could take a leap. She knew, without a doubt, that Sean would encourage her to leap. Because he'd be there to catch her. That's who he was. And she was starting to believe that he was really hers. If she couldn't take the leap now, she might never do it.

So, she'd be brave.

Feeling comfortable and a little giddy with the decision, she stepped out of the shower, hastily toweling off. She wanted to open up the spreadsheet she'd started of paramedic training programs. When she'd started it, she'd only considered the financial costs of the programs. Now she wanted to do some more research on the locations and what sort of job options might be available for him. If they went, they went together.

Delaney pulled up short at the sight of the figure on her couch.

Val gave a little wave. "Sorry. I saw you get back, and I wanted to bring over a sample of the new scents." She gestured toward the row of jar candles on the counter. "When you didn't answer, I let myself in. The door was unlocked."

Well, it's probably a good thing Sean was smart enough to save the getting naked for somewhere else.

She wrapped the towel more firmly around herself and went to grab some clothes from the bureau. "I was desperate for a shower."

"You're in a good mood."

Yeah, two days of mind-blowing sex will do that for you. Sean was an attentive, enthusiastic, and endlessly inventive lover. She'd have been lying if she didn't admit she was already dreaming of having him again, preferably in a bed this time. Hers. His. She wasn't picky.

"We had a good weekend." And if she took a bit longer to pull on her clean T-shirt in order to hide the blush that understatement evoked, who could blame her?

"Ah, *that* kind of good weekend. Good for you." The words were right, but something in Val's tone seemed off.

Delaney tugged on the rest of her clothes before turning to face her. "What?"

"What what?"

"I know that look. There's something you're not saying."

"It's nothing."

Delaney only lifted a brow.

Val huffed. "Okay, fine. It's just—don't you think you and Sean are moving a little fast? I mean, you've only been together a few weeks, and you've been spending every waking minute together. And now you're actually hot and heavy. Shouldn't you maybe slow things down? I mean… things went fast with Bryce, too, and that was… well. We both know what that was."

A train wreck, that's what.

"First, I've grown up a lot since Bryce. Second, Sean and I were friends first, so this really isn't that fast." Sean had said that himself, and he was right. Because Val still seemed worried, Delaney crossed over and plopped down on the sofa. "I appreciate you're concerned, but Sean is nothing like Bryce. He's such a better man. He's good for me."

"He makes you smile. That's really nice to see. You haven't smiled enough the last couple of years."

"I haven't felt like I had reason to until him."

"That's great." Her words were right, but her tone fell flat.

"Then why doesn't it sound like you actually think that's true?"

"It's just... I'm worried he's not good for you."

"Why wouldn't Sean be good for me?"

"You've been through so much stress the last few weeks with all this crap from the fires. And yet here you are, all kinds of happy and energetic, with an obviously hyped-up sex drive. I'm just concerned you're starting another manic episode."

Irritation dimmed some of that happy. "Aunt Val, I know you worry. And yeah, I do have all those symptoms right now, but I'm not manic. Plenty of normal people go through the same thing every day. It's called falling in love."

Val's eyes went wide. "I didn't know things had gotten that serious."

Had they? The idea of it made Delaney's

belly jump with nerves. Lust and very serious like was only a hop, skip, and a jump from love. Or maybe just a trip and a fall. God, Sean could make that so easy. She didn't know how she felt about that. Which was more terrifying—losing control in another manic episode or legitimately falling in love?

"I think… we're headed in that direction," she said carefully.

"Are you seeing him tonight?"

"No. He's on call for the fire department."

Her aunt brightened at that. "Then how about we have dinner and a movie night, just us girls? I've got chicken tikka masala in the crock pot."

It was a favorite pastime of theirs, something they'd done often until Delaney started dating Sean. But she really wanted to get started on more research. "Oh, I was going to catch up on some stuff."

Val's face fell, and she closed off. "It's fine. I can just freeze the rest and watch a movie by myself."

Guilt wormed its way through Delaney's excitement. She *had* been spending all her spare time with Sean. She really needed to have some one-on-one with Val. The spreadsheet could wait until later.

"I can put my stuff off. Is there coconut rice?"

Val's eyes brightened, and her lips curved in an indulgent smile. "Of course. I'll even make up some naan."

"You're too good to me."

"Nothing's too good for my favorite niece."

Delaney laughed and swung her feet to the floor. "I'm your only niece."

"You'd still be my favorite, even if I had half a dozen. C'mon. Let's go get started on that bread."

BECAUSE OF THE DROUGHT, Ben had the entire Wishful Volunteer Fire Department on rotating shifts at the fire station. Just a couple of guys on to speed things up when they caught some action. It had been a wise move, one that had given them critical minutes on at least three separate fires. Overnights at the station weren't like living in the barracks during fire season, but it gave Sean back that feeling of camaraderie, even if it was just Ben on duty with him tonight. That made up for the fact that he wasn't spending yet another night with Delaney. They both had to come up for air—and rest—sometime.

With a half-empty bottle of root beer and a nearly demolished double cheeseburger with everything at his elbow, Sean stared at the cards in his hand. They should've been in bed, but after a medical call and a minor brush fire from some local who didn't think the burn ban applied to him, they'd opted for an exceptionally late dinner and poker. Texas Hold 'em was more fun with more people, but he figured he could relieve his friend of some beer money for when the shift was over. Across the raggedy kitchen table that began its life in the fellowship hall of one of the local churches, Ben discarded two cards from his hand and drew two more.

"You know, this is the most relaxed I've seen you since you moved here."

If Sean was any more relaxed, he'd have been oozing onto the floor. His body was loose and well-used. "Guess I am."

"You usually have this whole restless thing going on. Even when we're out on calls, you're usually amped up, ready for more action than we actually get. And I can't remember the last time I saw you without your map."

"I've still got it." His big boss hadn't budged beyond manning the towers, but Sean was still monitoring conditions and marking the high threat areas. If something went wrong, it would save time in making a game plan to deal with the problem.

"I know you miss your hot shot crew. You have from the get-go, but this is the first time I don't think that's gnawing at you."

Sean realized it was true. "Guess it's not."

Face sober, Ben tossed in a couple more

chips. "Does that have something to do with a certain redhead?"

Tension snapped into those liquid muscles. Was he about to say something against Delaney? "Maybe."

The serious expression cracked into a smile. "I think it's great. Getting a girl, setting down some roots. Means you're looking at an actual life here. You look happy."

Sean relaxed again, letting out a controlled breath. Jesus, if that kind of apprehension was even a fraction of what Delaney dealt with on a daily basis, no wonder she hated being in public. What did it say that he felt it on her behalf now?

"I am happy. Mostly. I'm close enough to home to see family easily. I've got a solid job I like, the chance to eat smoke here, and I'm with an interesting, beautiful woman."

"You miss eating smoke full time."

"I'd be lying if I said I didn't."

"What if you had the chance to do that again?"

Sean's interest sharpened. "You know something I don't?"

"As fire chief, I've been having all sorts of meetings with the mayor and city council, discussing the needs of the city. After all the action we've caught this summer because of the drought, there's no question we need a full-time fire department. Scraping together enough from the budget to hire me was a big deal, and part of why they did it was to have someone in a position to make recommendations on how we can work our way towards that. Obviously, first priority has to be upgrading equipment, but Norah—the city planner, Norah Crawford —and I are working on some grants to do more. There's a lot of funding out there, and we hope to secure enough to make a real start in hiring people. I'd like to think you'll be around when we get to that point because I'd love to bring you on. Interested?"

"Hell yeah. What kind of timeline are we looking at?"

"Don't know yet. We've got a few in already

that we ought to hear something about by the end of the year."

Except at the end of the year, there was a chance he and Delaney would be moving.

"I don't know if I'll be here after the end of the year."

Ben frowned. "I thought we just established you were putting down roots."

"Delaney wants to train as a paramedic. WCC doesn't have that program, so she'll have to go somewhere else for a couple years to do it. If she goes, I'm probably going with her."

"That serious already?"

Sean waited for the twist of doubt in his gut, but it never came. "Yeah. I'll be introducing her to my family soon." She'd panic at that, so he'd have to ease her into the idea.

"Wow. Congrats, man."

"Thanks. I got lucky finding her."

"I could use some luck in that department."

Sean grinned. "You could let Norah do the bachelor auction. You never know. Miss Right might bid on you."

"Or the Casserole Patrol will buy me and expect me to pole dance or some shit."

Snorting, Sean laid down his straight and raked in the pot. As they set up for the next hand, he asked, "Has there been any more news on the arson case while I was gone?"

"Nah. Whoever did it probably won't get caught without making a mistake."

"Which means setting another fire." Sean tipped back his root beer. "I've been worried about that. I was willing to buy the fire at Gina Draper's house as an accident until the second one in her boyfriend's car. But taken together, it seems like the start of a pattern. There's no consistency of method, but you've got consistency of target—in both cases, Bryce Kelso. His home. His vehicle."

"What's the motive?"

"He's a shit of a human being, with a history of pissing people off. He cheated on Delaney when they were together. Chances are, if he hasn't already, he'll cheat on Gina."

"Once a cheater, always a cheater," Ben agreed. "You think Gina could've done it?"

Sean considered. "Obviously, she had means and opportunity with the house fire. And before that, she came after Delaney at work. Evidently, she'd got wind that Delaney was seen with Bryce at The Mudcat a few days before. There was a big public scene that proves unequivocally that Gina is the jealous type."

"Yeah, but do you really buy her as an arsonist?"

"I buy her as a jealous bitch. Hell hath no fury like a woman scorned and all that. If we figure out who Bryce is sniffing around or who he might be pissing off, chances are, we'll find either the perpetrator or the motive or both."

"We?"

"Well, not we in particular. We don't have any kind of authority on that front. But I don't see why we can't put our heads together to think up some suggestions of avenues the police department hasn't checked yet."

"Fair enough."

The alerts hit their phones simultaneously. Shoving back from the table, Sean checked the readout.

Involved structure fire 589B Hughes St.

And for the first time in his career fighting fire, utter terror washed over him. 589B was Delaney's apartment.

CHAPTER 8

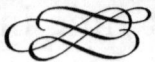

*D*elaney tipped her head back, exposing her throat for more of the nibbling kisses Sean trailed across her skin. "Mmm, that's nice. Hawaii was such a great idea."

"A last hurrah before you start back school," he murmured. His hands skimmed along her ribs, around to the hook of her bikini top. He flicked it open, drawing it down her arms, leaving her breasts exposed to the tropical air—and his mouth.

Her breath came shorter. "I like your idea of a last hurrah."

"Making love by a waterfall has been on my list." The roar of it nearly drowned out his words.

Delaney threaded her fingers through the hair at his nape as he licked and suckled, until she felt an answering tug deeper, lower. "I really like that list. Maybe we should shift into the water, though. It's a lot hotter than I thought Hawaii would be."

"In a minute." He worked his way down her torso, fingers hooking into the sides of her bikini bottoms and drawing them down.

Sweat slicked her skin, and she moved restlessly as he settled his broad shoulders between her legs. "Much as I really want you to do what you're about to do, I'm actually getting overheated in a not good way. Let's get into the water."

Sean rested his cheek against her thigh as he stared up her body. "We could hit the shower. Shower sex is on the list, too."

"That's a definite yes when we get back to the bungalow." As soon as she said the words, they were there, and it wasn't a grassy bank beneath her back, but a chaise lounge. "What the—?"

Dreaming, she realized. *Dreaming and hot. Did the AC go out?*

Dragging herself out of the depths of sleep, Delaney forced her eyes open. The heat and roar came with her, out of the dream. It was too bright. Morning already? Disoriented, she sat up in bed—and saw the flames.

Consciousness slammed into her, even as she coughed from the billowing smoke. For a moment she could only stare, dumbfounded, at the beast she'd heard Sean call the dragon crawling across her apartment.

Sean. Fire. Move.

She rolled out of bed and hit the floor, knowing she needed to stay low. The wood beneath her knees was hot. Too hot. Was the fire in the garage below? Her body felt uncoordinated and slow. Too much wine with dinner. She was still a little tipsy. Or maybe that was oxygen deprivation. Grabbing a discarded t-shirt from a chair, she covered her mouth and tried not to breathe too deep. She had to get to the door. But even as she headed in that direction, flames leapt from the wall of the kitchen and raced across the ceiling. Cinders fell, igniting the sofa and effectively blocking her way.

The bathroom. There was a small window in there that opened onto a hackberry tree. Maybe she could get out that way, or at least wet herself down. The smoke was getting thicker, darker. She couldn't quite see, but she bellied toward the tiny bathroom, feeling her hands and knees searing, as if she were crawling along the hot concrete of the city pool at the peak of a summer afternoon. No time to search for more clothes to protect her.

In the bathroom she pushed to her feet, fighting with the window over the bathtub. "Come on. Come *on!*" But no matter how hard she shoved, she couldn't get the sash to budge. Panic clawed up her spine.

Stay calm. Find another way.

Delaney switched on the shower full blast, spending precious seconds stepping under the spray, soaking herself to the skin. She realized as she raced out of the bathroom that it had been a mistake. In those few minutes, the fire had spread, licking across the floor until her collection of area rugs went up like matchsticks.

For one hysterical moment, she thought of the game she'd played as a kid, where she'd imagined the living room floor covered with lava. She'd used couch cushions and chairs as little islands of safety. But there were no islands of safety, and she couldn't make it to any of the other windows.

Frantic, she searched for something she could use to break the glass in the bathroom. The smoke was too thick. She couldn't breathe. She bolted back into the bathroom and beat at the window. But her hands only bounced off the glass. Each blow was weaker than the last. In some distant part of her mind, she recognized the smoke was getting to her. If she didn't get the window broken, didn't get out, she wouldn't make it out. But even as the thought crossed her mind, she was sinking to her knees in the tub, unable to hold herself upright.

Sean. I'm sorry. I'm sorry we had so little time.

Somehow, she'd known they wouldn't last. But she'd expected him to walk away, not to be pulled away from him by a cruel twist of fate. This would crush him. He'd blame himself, believe that somehow, he should have known. Should've been able to stop this.

You can't stop karma. This is clearly mine.

At the sound of splintering wood, Delaney instinctively covered her head, expecting at any moment to be buried in flaming debris. But nothing landed on her. A few moments later, a figure filled the bathroom doorway, silhouetted by the raging fire beyond. For half a second, she expected to see wings spreading out behind him, as if he were some kind of avenging angel come to strike her down. When he stepped forward, she cringed back in the tub, her vision going gray. Then the shape of him came clearer, and she recognized the turnout gear and firefighter's helmet.

Lunging into the room, he scooped her up. Familiar gray-green eyes burned her from behind the mask.

Sean.

He'd come for her. Relief flooded her system. Delaney curled into him, her chest aching as she coughed. Her lungs burned and the taste of ash and chemicals coated her mouth. Every inch of skin felt hot and tight. But he'd come for her. Trusting he'd find a way out, she let herself slide into the black.

DELANEY SLUMPED AGAINST HIS CHEST.

No. No no no. Don't you fucking dare die on me.

Shoving the thought from his mind, Sean narrowed his focus to getting them both out of here alive. Even the path he'd taken from the door had been swallowed up as the dragon ate its fill. Clutching her close, he bolted, using every ounce of the agility he'd once honed on the football field. Twenty feet to the door. Fifteen. Ten.

His foot crashed through the floorboards. On a roar, he caught himself with his other leg, driving them forward, yanking himself free of the hole. The momentum propelled him out of the door so fast, he nearly took a header down the stairs. Jerking backward, he managed to shift the trajectory, so he landed hard on his ass on a tread and didn't drop Delaney.

Ben was already climbing toward Sean as he got to his feet. Sean shook his head, refusing to hand her over. He couldn't. He had to see to her himself. Dimly, he was aware that hoses were trained on both the garage apartment and the nearby house to keep it from catching. The rest of their team had the situation as under control as it could be. The entire structure was involved now, flames lighting up the night as he hustled across the yard and laid her out away from danger.

Val rushed up, hysterical. "Oh my God! Oh my God! Is she alive?"

Ben inserted himself, holding her back as Sean did his job, checking Delaney's breath and pulse. She had both.

Thank God.

But she didn't rouse under his ministrations. Sean covered her face with an oxygen mask, curling a hand around hers and waiting. For long minutes, the only thing he knew was the rise and fall of her chest.

"Come on. Come on, baby. Wake up." He didn't know what he'd do if she didn't.

When her eyes fluttered open, he all but wept in gratitude. Her eyes wheeled, her head lolling in confusion, trying to take in everything at once.

"Steady. Just stay still now and breathe. You're all right. Just breathe."

The fingers wrapped in his squeezed, and the adrenaline he'd been riding since the call came in finally crashed. Sean sank back, almost tumbling to the ground beside her. He'd nearly lost her. Overcome, he gathered her up, gently pulling her into his lap and rocking.

"You're okay. You're okay." He said it over and over, as much to reassure himself as her.

Delaney curled into him, one arm wrapping around his shoulders. The fear that had lodged in his chest loosened.

"Y'all might want this." Ben offered a blanket.

Sean took it, tucking it around her bare, dirty legs, despite the heat behind them. He realized the T-shirt she wore to sleep in was damp. "It's a fucking miracle you weren't more seriously burned."

"When I couldn't get out, I got in the shower," she rasped.

"That probably saved your life" Sean pressed his brow to hers, sending up prayers of thanks that she'd thought quickly and that he'd made it inside. Another minute and he wouldn't have been able to get her out.

"You saved my life." She laid a hand against his cheek, and Sean turned into the touch, needing the contact.

Something pulsed between them. Something greater than heat, deeper than affection, beyond respect. As the knowledge of it settled in his bones, he lifted his hand to mirror her gesture, cupping her face. He opened his mouth.

Val fell to her knees beside them, weeping. "Oh God. Oh God, why did you go home?"

The something would bear analyzing later, in the light of day, after they'd both processed everything that had happened. Sean rewound Val's words in his head and played them again. The oddity of her statement broke through his haze of relief. "What are you talking about?"

Delaney shoved the mask up fully. "I went to Val's for dinner. We had too much wine, so I went to sleep in the guest room after our movie."

Val picked up the thread. "I woke up to pee, and I saw the fire from my window. I called 911 to report it and went to wake you up and you weren't there, and I thought— God. God, I don't know what I'd do if I lost you!"

Delaney reached up to take her hand. "I woke up and wanted my own bed, so I stumbled home." A fit of coughing interrupted the explanation. "I don't know what started the fire. I guess I was sleeping extra hard because of the wine. If you hadn't seen the fire and called…" She trailed off, staring at her aunt with a mixture of gratitude and horror.

Val sobbed harder.

"It's okay. I'm okay," Delaney soothed.

"But all your things. Your apartment…"

A shadow crossed Delaney's face at that. Everything she had in the world had been in that apartment, and that hadn't been all that much. She'd lost everything in this fire. Still, she squeezed Val's hand. "It's just stuff. We can replace it. I'm alive, and I'm whole. That's the most important thing. It was all just a terrible accident."

Ben strode up behind them, catching Sean's eye—and he knew. "I've called in the fire marshal to confirm, but I can already tell you, this was no accident."

CHAPTER 9

"You were super lucky. Only minor burns, some bruises, and smoke inhalation. I'm prescribing a few days of rest, but there's no reason you can't come back to work by the end of the week."

Delaney managed a weak smile for Miranda, grateful she'd been the doctor on duty in the ER when she'd been brought in. "Thanks." She'd need the work now more than ever. Everything she owned had been in her apartment. Even the T-shirt she'd been wearing when Sean pulled her out was ruined. The hospital scrubs Miranda had unearthed for her were baggy and bunched around the ankles. Delaney had a little money put by in savings, money she'd intended to go toward moving expenses and tuition. Obviously more school was off the table for now. In the grand scheme of losses from the night, that was just more insult on top of considerable injury.

Get over yourself. You're alive and mostly unhurt. And your car wasn't in the garage. It could have been so much worse.

"I know you're eager to get some rest, so I'll get the discharge paperwork started. Where will you be staying?" Miranda asked.

"With me. Of course, she'll stay with me," Val said.

Delaney felt Sean tense beside her. She laid a hand on his arm and squeezed. That was not a conversation she wanted to have with an audience.

Miranda just nodded. "I'll be back in a little while. The cafeteria should be open now for breakfast in case y'all want anything while you wait."

Of course, it was. Because it was dawn, and they'd been here the rest of the night.

As soon as Miranda slipped out of the room, Delaney looked at her aunt. "I am actually pretty hungry."

"Of course, you are! I'll just run on down and pick something up for all of us."

"Biscuits would be awesome. Thanks, Aunt Val."

Once her footsteps faded, Sean shifted to sit on the bed beside Delaney, folding her hand in his. "I want you to come stay with me."

That he would offer made a little puddle of warmth in the ice locking down her emotions. She was due to fall apart good and proper in the not distant future, but she'd hold it together a while longer. The rough stubble of his cheek rasped her palm as she cupped his face. "I want to. You have no idea how much I want that." The prospect of falling asleep in his arms made her feel safe, and she wanted to be with him.

His lips pulled into a frown. "But?"

"For one, it's not fair to your roommate. But the bigger issue is that I have more than just myself to worry about. I can't leave Val alone. You saw her. She's just as shaken up about all this as I am. She's been stuck in a mental loop of how everything might've gone wrong."

"She's not the only one," he growled.

"But it didn't. Because of you. Everything's gonna be okay." How did she work her way around to being the one to reassure him?

Sean's expression turned mulish. "Everything's not okay. That fire was arson."

"We don't know that for sure yet." And God knew, she was clinging to the thin thread of hope that Ben was mistaken. Because if he wasn't…

"Actually, yeah we do." Ethan's voice came from the doorway. "Sorry to interrupt, but I figured you'd want confirmation as soon as we had it. Someone tampered with the old fuse box."

Though Delaney had been expecting *some-*

thing, Ethan's pronouncement hit her like a ton of bricks. "So, it really was arson?"

"Afraid so."

Someone had set her apartment on fire. Deliberately. Who hated her that much? Why? She knew she'd made mistakes in her life, but surely —*surely* none of them merited this kind of retaliation.

Sean's arm tightened around her. "What did Charlie say? Was it the kind of tampering that could've sparked at any time?"

Ethan gave him a measured look. "He said it probably sparked almost immediately."

Sean's body hardened. "So, this wasn't just arson, it was attempted murder."

Murder?

The ugly word crashed over Delaney like a wave, spawning an instant denial. "What? But that's ridiculous," she sputtered. "Who would want to kill me?"

Ethan sank into the visitor's chair in the corner of the hospital room. "Was it widely known you weren't supposed to be home last night?"

"I… no. I'd been gone all weekend for a spontaneous trip with Sean, and I had dinner with my aunt. There was no reason for anybody to believe I wouldn't be home after that. I just live —lived right there. If I hadn't overdone it on the wine, I'd have just gone home after the movie."

"Where was Gina Draper?" Sean demanded.

Gina? She was a hateful bitch, but this?

"Allegedly home in bed with Bryce. I checked with them before I came up here. The fact is, we've got three fires. You were implicated in two, targeted in the third. Is there somebody who's a common enemy for all three of you?"

The idea of it was ludicrous. "Nobody I can think of. We don't run in the same circles."

"This fire is a big escalation from the first two," Sean said. "Neither of the first ones were life threatening."

"And I assure you, we're taking that seriously. I'll be posting an officer on your residence until we get to the bottom of this. Where will you be staying?"

"With my aunt."

"I'm staying, too," Sean announced.

Delaney's mouth fell open.

"I'll sleep on the sofa if Val has a problem with me being there, but you need protection."

"I think it's a good idea," Ethan agreed.

"What's going on?" Val came back into the room, her cheeks losing a few shades of color as she saw Ethan.

"They confirmed arson," Sean said.

Val laid a hand over her heart. "Who would do such a thing?"

"We don't know yet. But finding out is our top priority," Ethan told her.

Miranda came back into the room, paperwork in hand. Her expression darkened at the sight of her boyfriend. "If you're here, it's bad news."

"Afraid so. Arson."

"Have you asked Delaney everything you have to?"

"For now."

"Good. Because she needs rest. And minimal talking the rest of the day. Doctor's orders."

He nodded and for one second broke the stoic cop mask. "I'll see you at home, Doc."

Miranda nodded. "Be careful."

"Always." With a quick nod to the rest of them, he said, "I'll be in touch."

Miranda laid a hand over Delaney's. "He'll find whoever's behind this. He's a good cop."

"I know. Right now, I just… can't think about it anymore. I'm exhausted."

"Rest."

As Miranda went over the remaining discharge instructions, they ate the sausage biscuits Val had brought back from the cafeteria, though Delaney's appetite had fled.

"I'll call to check on you later, okay?"

She nodded and slid off the bed, slipping on the flip-flops someone had unearthed in the lost and found.

Val put an arm around her. "Let's get you home and tucked into bed. It'll be just like old times."

It wouldn't, but Delaney had to smile at her aunt's effort to make her feel better. "With the addition of a bodyguard."

Val paused. "What?"

"Sean's staying with us while the police sort this out."

"I don't like the two of you alone in that house after all this. I'm gonna see you're both safe."

"Well, aren't you a sweet boy?" Val gave Delaney a little squeeze and dropped her voice a notch. "I think you found a keeper this time."

She found she could smile a little as she met Sean's eyes. "Yeah, I think I did, too."

SEAN WHEELED his truck into the drive behind Delaney's little compact car. His eyes automatically tracked to the blackened remains of her garage apartment. There wasn't much left. Just the lower portion of the north and west walls. Everything else had been reduced to rubble. He wondered if Val would rebuild once the insurance money came in. Of course, that was all tied up until the arson investigation was closed. Wanting a progress report, he strode over to the police cruiser parked across the street.

Clint Yarbrough rolled the window down. "Evenin'."

"Hey Clint. Any updates?"

"Nope. Everything's been quiet. Chief's waiting on the results of some tests at the state crime lab. We all know how long that kind of thing takes. It'll probably be a while before we know something, unless our firestarter strikes again."

"Let's hope he doesn't." But Sean had little hope of that. He'd been around fire all his adult life. His gauge of the whole situation was that their perpetrator had figured out he liked fire. Each one had been bigger than the one before.

Sean didn't like to think about what the next step up might be.

Giving Clint a wave, he headed inside. Today had been Delaney's first day back at work. Had it gone well? Had she overdone? Had she been harassed? Surely in the wake of the fire, no one could possibly think she was anything other than another victim.

The sight of tears streaming down her cheeks had him revising that assessment and fighting a burst of temper. "What happened?"

She waved a hand and smiled up at him. "No, no, it's a good cry. Everybody at work took up a collection to help me replace all the essentials."

Happy tears. Sean shifted gears, dropping down onto the sofa beside her and tugging her into his arms. "Oh, well, of course they did." It was a good thing, the right thing to do. But how often had the good and right thing been applied to her in this town? Sean understood what this meant to her. Acceptance by a group of women she respected. Friendship.

He pressed a kiss to her temple and glanced toward the kitchen and Val. A ripple of irritation crossed her features as she cleared the detritus that had accumulated on the table. He'd learned even in just a few days that she didn't like the pile up. Not even a shopping bag and a few envelopes and junk mail fliers. He decided it was a good thing he hadn't brought much stuff and that he was keeping it all confined to the room he shared with Delaney.

"Something smells awesome," he called.

"Chicken lasagna with garlic bread. It'll be ready soon."

Feeling the specter of his mother hanging over one shoulder, reminding him of his manners, Sean asked, "What can I do to help? Set the table? Put ice in the glasses?"

"Nothing. I've got it." There was nothing inherently wrong with her words, but her tone was just a shade too brusque. Val wasn't happy with him being here.

As they ate supper—turned out chicken lasagna was one of Delaney's favorites—Sean thought about what she'd said about how Val missed her and was jealous of the time the two of them spent together. Wanting to be inclusive, he asked, "How would you ladies like to have a game night after dinner?"

"I'm not in the mood for games," Val said, already clearing her plate.

"How about a movie then? Delaney tells me you make amazing popcorn."

"Oh, a movie sounds good," Delaney agreed. "How about it, Aunt Val?"

"You two go on. I think I'm gonna read tonight."

Shot down again. So far, the older woman had rejected all his overtures. Maybe part of it was because they didn't see eye to eye on what was best for Delaney. Val seemed determined to coddle her, where Sean was all about helping her regain some sense of control and normalcy.

"Are you feeling okay?" Delaney asked.

"Why wouldn't I be?"

"Well, we've kinda been through a lot this week. The stress is pretty intense."

Val's gaze sharpened. "Are *you* feeling okay? Sleeping all right?"

It wasn't the first time she'd asked. Could she not see how those questions, designed to fish for whether Delaney was on the verge of another swing, annoyed her niece?

"I'm fine. Better than expected. But, yeah, I'm seeing my therapist after everything that happened. I just thought maybe you'd like to talk to somebody, too."

Val visibly prickled at the suggestion. "I don't need to see anybody." She slipped her rinsed plate into the dishwasher and shut it with a definitive click. "I'm going to go read. You two enjoy each other."

"We'll do the dishes," Sean called.

At the sound of Val's bedroom door closing with a thunk, Delaney let out a sigh. "Well, that went over like a lead balloon. I can't get her to see that therapy would be good for her. Normal. Especially after an upset like this."

"You've tried before?"

Delaney cleared her own plate. "Sure. She's

got issues. She's not the family black sheep by choice any more than I am."

Sean joined her in the kitchen, automatically filling the sink with soapy water and falling into the rhythm of doing dishes with her. "What happened there?"

"I don't know. Neither she nor my parents will talk about it."

Sean wondered why. Then again, he wondered a lot about Delaney's family. He couldn't wrap his brain around the idea that they'd cut their daughter off for two years. "Have you heard from your parents?"

"They called yesterday, mad that I hadn't called myself." She rolled her eyes as she swiped water off a skillet. "But I guess it was a wake-up call. They want to see me."

"Do you want to see them?" He studied her face as she considered the question. She was very matter of fact about her relationship with her parents most of the time, but he knew their rejection had hurt her. That they'd reached out after all this might be the beginning of a bridge between them. For her sake, he hoped so.

"I don't know. I guess I won't know until I go and see how it goes. I put them off a couple of days."

"Do you want me to go with you?" Maybe they'd behave better if she came with a buffer.

Delaney turned into him, sliding her arms around his waist, despite his soapy hands. "That's sweet, but I think I need to do this on my own."

"Offer stands."

"Right now, what I'd really like to do is hole up in our room, put on a movie and make out." To emphasize the point, she ran her hands down his back and grabbed his ass.

Our room. Sean liked the sound of that. He liked it a whole helluva lot. He grinned as he stepped into her, letting her know exactly what that did to him. "I do like the way you think."

"Let me just prep this money for a bank deposit tomorrow while you finish that casserole dish."

He plunged his hands into the water and scrubbed with renewed vigor.

"Where did it go?"

Sean looked up. "Where did you leave it?"

"It was in an envelope right here on the kitchen table."

"Val cleared everything for dinner."

"Maybe she stuck it in my room." She headed down the hall to check.

Sean was drying the casserole dish when he heard her knocking on Val's door.

"Hey, did you see a plain white envelope on the kitchen table when you were clearing up for dinner?"

"No. All I saw was some junk mail and the Dollar General bag. I tossed the junk."

Sean opened the garbage and rifled through the contents in case the envelope was accidentally mixed in. "Not in the trash."

"Are you sure you brought it home?" Val asked. "Maybe you left it at work or in your car?"

Delaney slipped outside to look in her car.

She came back a minute later, empty-handed. "Not there either. Maybe I *did* leave it at work. I'll check tomorrow. Man, I hope I didn't lose that."

"Don't worry about it. I'll spot you if you need it," Val offered.

"It's less about that and more that they're all trying to help me, and I'd hate for that to be for nothing because I was inadvertently careless. But thank you. I really appreciate you looking out for me and giving me a place to live —again."

"Of course. That's what family is for."

Sean followed Delaney into their room. She pulled up Netflix. "What do you want to watch?"

"Does it matter?"

It was her turn to grin. "I suppose not."

While she flipped over to where they'd left off with the latest Marvel series, Sean's mind was on her aunt.

That envelope had been on the table. He'd seen it. Did Val really not remember seeing it, or was there more to the story? What if she was into something? In some kind of trouble. Did she need the money herself? If she did, why would she offer to spot Delaney?

He didn't have any answers. As Delaney crawled up the bed and snuggled against him, he decided he'd sleep on it. If the money didn't turn up tomorrow, he'd talk to Delaney about it. She had enough to worry about right this second, and he had a warm, willing woman to please.

CHAPTER 10

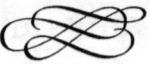

*D*elaney felt positively sick. The envelope of donations wasn't at the clinic. Deep down, she'd known it wouldn't be. She *knew* she'd taken it home yesterday. What had happened to the money? It *had* to be somewhere in the house. She'd tear everything apart if she had to. Val and Sean would help.

His truck was in the drive when she got home. Val's car was nowhere to be seen. Maybe she'd stopped by the grocery. Ever since the fire, she'd been on a kick of making all of Delaney's favorites. It was sweet and seemed to make her feel better about the situation they all found themselves in.

Sean was waiting in the living room, perched on the sofa, his hands loosely clasped between his knees. His grim expression set off all kinds of alarm bells and had anxiety spiking.

"What is it? What's wrong? Did they find the arsonist? Has there been another fire?"

"Come sit down. I need to talk to you." He patted the cushion beside him.

Is he about to break up with me? The idea of it terrified her. But no. This was Sean. Her Sean. If he'd been planning to break up, he wouldn't have moved in for guard duty. He wouldn't be warming her bed.

Taking a breath, Delaney forced her trembling legs to carry her over to him. His big, strong fingers curled around hers as she sat, and Delaney felt herself steady.

"I think I know what happened to the money."

Relief drowned out some of the anxiety. "Oh good. Because it's not at the clinic."

"That's because you left it on the table, exactly as you said. Val did move it. I saw her do it as she was setting the table."

I knew I wasn't crazy. "And put it where?"

"I don't know."

"She must not have seen it among all the junk mail."

He took a breath. "I'm pretty sure she saw it, honey. And I'm pretty sure she took it."

"What? That's ridiculous." She must not have heard him right.

"Is it? Listen. Without that money, you're more dependent on her. You said yourself she loves being needed. I don't think she wants you to have any outside help."

"There's a big damned difference—" She yanked her hand away, wondering where the hell this was coming from. "—between liking to do stuff for people and what you're suggesting."

"There's more, and you aren't going to like it."

He'd just accused her aunt of theft. How much worse could it get?

"I think there's a strong possibility she set the fire."

A lot worse, apparently. Delaney couldn't even stay sitting next to him. She shot to her feet, defensive temper rolling through her in waves. "You're out of your mind."

"Not to hurt you," he said quickly. "I don't think she ever intended that. But to make you dependent on her again. To get you back in her house. Think about it. She deliberately plied you with wine. More than you usually drink. She made sure—she thought—that you were out of the apartment that night. When I got you out, she was beside herself. She asked why you went home, as if that wasn't the plan, wasn't what she'd counted on."

What kind of Twilight Zone was he living in? "She asked that because she didn't know I'd left the house. She was scared for my life."

"She was scared she'd killed or hurt you."

"My aunt loves me," Delaney snapped. The

words, the allegations, were beyond ugly. And they just weren't true. Delaney *knew* Val loved her. She was the only person she'd been able to count on to love her, no matter what.

"She does. But it's a twisted, dependent sort of love. She keeps trying to bring you back to the nest. She's hated you getting more independent. You said yourself you were worried about leaving her. And that she's got some long-standing mental health issues that remain unaddressed. I think you're right, and I think she'll do anything to keep you with her."

Her sweet, supportive, understanding Sean was leveling the exact same kind of accusations at her aunt that others had thrown at her. It was beyond ludicrous. He'd been so good to her, so good for her. He wasn't that guy. "You can't honestly believe this."

There had to be some missing piece. Some explanation that would clear this up.

"I don't make the accusation lightly, but I've been trying to figure this out, piece together what I know, what I've seen, and make it make some kind of sense. I know you're close, but I've watched her with you. She doesn't like me, and she's jealous of the time we spend together. She doesn't like that I encourage you to take those leaps to get out on your own."

Delaney closed her eyes and shook her head, wishing she could just make all of this stop. But his words kept coming.

"Every step you take toward independence, toward leaving, she tries to counter. She's controlling you through guilt and obligation. She's been manipulating you to stay. And when it looked like that wasn't going to cut it, she got desperate."

"How dare you? She let you in our house. Fed you. She's been kind to you. And you accuse her of *this?* It's bullshit. You're imagining threats where there are none."

"I know you don't want to think about this. I know you're angry. And I hope like hell I'm wrong. But you need to know, one way or the

KAIT NOLAN

other. We need to search her room while she's gone."

"I will do no such thing." She'd never violate Val's privacy like that.

Sean continued as if she hadn't spoken. "We need to see if the money's there. If we find it, we'll have confirmation."

"Confirmation of *what* exactly?"

He scooped a hand through his hair and blew out a frustrated breath. "Confirmation that she's not who you think she is. That you can't trust her."

That she's crazy.

He didn't say it, but Delaney heard it anyway. The same way she'd heard it when people said it about her. But she'd never expected to hear it from him. She'd thought he was different. But when push came to shove, he was just like everyone else.

"Get out."

Eyes stricken, he reached for her. "Delaney, please."

She dodged him, not wanting to feel those

170

hands that had brought her comfort and pleasure. "No. I know you want answers as badly as I do, but you have no right to say the exact things about her that people have said about me. I won't stand here and listen to that."

His head kicked back as if she'd slapped him, horror skating over his features. His voice was barely more than a stunned whisper. "It's not the same thing."

But it was. And she'd promised herself she'd never just endure that kind of thing again. Especially not from him. "You need to go."

"I'm just trying to protect you."

Delaney crossed her arms over her chest. She should've been protecting herself from him. "Val's not going to hurt me. But you sure as hell have."

His hands curled into fists, but he didn't move. "I don't want to leave you alone with her."

"You don't get a choice here. I want you to go. I need you to go." Before she fell to pieces.

After a long moment of silence, he moved to

the front door and opened it. Delaney couldn't watch.

"If you need anything, I'll come."

She said nothing.

"Search her room. Get the truth," he said again.

The sound of the door closing made her flinch. On a silent sob, she dropped to her knees where she stood.

She'd known, on some level, that they wouldn't last. But he'd made her believe they stood a chance. More than that, he'd made her believe they were right for each other. But no one who was right for her could be so utterly disrespectful to Val. No one who was right could ever use her mental health problems to justify these accusations. And that simply meant that he wasn't right for her.

The truth of that broke the heart that he'd begun to heal.

∾

THE ONLY REASON Sean could actually walk out the door was the police cruiser parked across the street. That and the fact that he truly didn't think Val wanted to physically harm Delaney. As he climbed into his truck, he wondered if that could've possibly gone any worse. There was no *good* way to reveal his suspicions. He could've gone straight to the police and let them investigate, but it had felt like more of a betrayal to blindside Delaney. Clearly, she didn't see it that way.

He'd thought… well, he didn't know what he'd thought. That they'd talk it out? Search the house for the money together? He hadn't expected her to throw him out. And that was just stupidity on his part. He was, in essence, attacking the primary person she trusted. And he'd been fool enough to think it would be okay because she trusted *him.* Obviously, family was more important than whatever was between them.

Sean slammed his hands against the steering wheel, furious with himself, with the situation.

He should've found another way. Should have taken the time to better support his theories. Something. Anything to have stopped Delaney from looking at him like he'd stabbed her through the heart.

The last thing Sean ever wanted to do was hurt her. She'd had more than enough of that in her lifetime. Couldn't she see he was doing this because he cared about her?

You're imagining threats where there are none.

Was he doing that? Sean was willing to admit he enjoyed being her hero—saving her, taking care of her in a million little ways. But he wasn't manufacturing threats that weren't there. He hadn't imagined the fire that had nearly taken her life.

Should he go to the police now? What if he was wrong? His gut said he wasn't, but he didn't exactly have a smoking gun. Just a lot of supposition. If he went to the police and Val wasn't behind it, how was he any different from the people who'd accused Delaney? He hadn't considered it that way before, but he *was* using the same arguments that had been used against her.

Needing a second opinion, Sean headed across town.

Ben answered the door. "Dude, you look like shit. What's wrong?"

"So much."

Ben jerked his head. "Come in. I'll get you a beer."

Out of habit, Sean took the Abita, but he didn't actually drink.

"Did you and Delaney have a fight?"

The humorless laugh burst out. "You could say that. I just accused her aunt of setting the fire."

Ben stared at him over the fridge door. "You did what?" He grabbed his own beer, twisting off the top. "Tell me exactly what happened."

So he did. By the time he'd finished, he'd peeled the label off the bottle and torn it to shreds.

"Shit, man. Did you go to the police?"

"Not yet. That's why I'm here. Am I out of line? Is my judgment compromised?"

"Well, tell me this—why did you assume this was about Delaney rather than about the money? Burning down property for the insurance is a pretty classic reason for arson. And you already said Val took the donations from Delaney's coworkers."

"It'd be pretty dumb to set a fire that was blatant arson to try to scam insurance. I don't think Val's stupid. And I don't think she'd get enough for that garage to do much, even if the payout wasn't all tied up because of the investigation."

"That's speculation."

"All of it is speculation. It's instinct. Intuition or whatever the hell. Their relationship just isn't quite right. She says the right things, seems to do the right things, but there's just something off about it. Delaney doesn't see it because she's so grateful for the help Val gave her, she can't fathom there'd be anything behind that but love. Her family screwed her over two years ago, so I think that's made her even closer to Val than she would've been."

Ben tipped back his beer. "Do you think Val could be behind the other fires?"

Sean hadn't considered it before, but he did now. "I have no idea if Val had an opportunity. But motive?" His fingers drummed against the bottle. "If we stick to the theory that this is all about Delaney, then the first fire could've been revenge on Gina for coming after Delaney again. Val was at the clinic when that went down. And the car fire could've been revenge against Bryce for sniffing around again."

"I think it's reasonable enough suspicion that the police ought to check into her whereabouts for both fires."

Sean said nothing, finally taking a sip of his now lukewarm beer.

"You don't look convinced," Ben observed.

"I just… I don't want to make another mistake here. I don't want to go pointing more fingers without solid justification."

"I think your gut is justification. You're not

prone to flights of fancy. But if you want to, take the night and sleep on it. If your theory about Val's motives is accurate, then she's gotten what she wanted— Delaney in her house, all to herself. So, your girl should be safe."

"I'm not sure she's my girl anymore after all this." It hurt to admit that and to know it was all his fault.

"She's upset, and she's pissed. There wasn't really any way around that in this situation. But you don't know what side she'll come down on when the dust settles. If you're right and the police prove it..." He trailed off.

"There's no good outcome to this, Ben. Delaney's going to be hurt either way. Either I'm right and her aunt is mentally unstable and dangerous, which will crush her because Val is the only family she really has now. Or I'm wrong, and I get lumped in with all the other assholes who judge people based on their mental health issues."

"It's a shit situation for damned sure. But the

best outcome to hope for here is the one where the woman you love is safe."

Sean stared at him, his heart thudding against his ribs with the same kind of adrenaline spike he felt before heading into a fire. "I didn't say I loved her."

Ben just lifted a brow. "Brother, you didn't have to. You don't look at changing your whole life for a woman after a few months unless you love her."

"And you have so much experience with this through your perennially single status?"

"I wasn't always single." He clapped Sean on the shoulder. "Go home. Sleep on it. And if you think it's the right thing, take it to the police tomorrow. In the meantime, do me a favor and watch your back. You may be fine since you and Delaney are on the outs right now, but you've said yourself Val doesn't like you. If she's behind all this other stuff… could be she decides to exact a little payback from you, too."

"There's a cheerful thought."

"You can't be too careful."

"I'll keep my eyes open. Thanks for listening, man."

"Anytime."

Feeling clearer-headed, if not actually better, Sean headed home for the first time in a week to figure out if he had a chance in hell of saving his relationship.

CHAPTER 11

Why had she agreed to brunch with her parents? Delaney didn't want to go. She'd been awake most of the night crying. Oh, and hiding the reason for Sean's absence from Val. Because if she admitted they broke up, Val would want to know why, and no way in hell was Delaney sharing those hurtful suspicions. She'd told her aunt he had to be up and out early for work. Not a lie. He was making up for some time off by working Saturday. She'd seen it on his work schedule, which was among the stuff he'd left behind. She was exhausted and tender and didn't relish getting all that back to him. Maybe she could get someone to drop it off for her, so she didn't have to see him.

Before Delaney could give that idea any further consideration, the front door of her childhood home swung open, and a kitchen towel nearly slapped her in the face as Bridget threw her arms around Delaney's shoulders in a bonecracking hug. Delaney didn't move, partly because she actually couldn't breathe and partly because she had no idea what to do with this behavior. She hadn't received a shred of affection from her parents since the diagnosis, so this welcome the prodigal daughter home routine was just plain weird.

"Oh honey, we're so happy you came." Bridget stepped back, dragging Delaney into the house. "Wallace, she's here!"

Delaney's dad emerged from the den and pulled her into a looser but equally awkward hug.

"Um, hi, Dad."

"I already laid brunch out," Bridget babbled, gesturing toward the kitchen.

Knowing it was too late to bolt, Delaney followed, taking in the new sofa and the different paint color in the den. Life had gone on without her. She shouldn't be surprised or hurt over it, but somehow seeing the changes was a fresh slice to her already bruised heart.

"—made eggs Benedict and a fresh fruit salad. There's coffee. Or tea if you'd prefer."

Delaney had agreed to this meal with intentions of being cordial and positive, seeing where things went. But faced with this farce of formality, she found she didn't have the patience. Curling her hands around the back of a kitchen chair, she pinned her mother with a hard stare. "Why am I here? You've wanted nothing to do with me for two years."

Her mom buried her face in the kitchen towel and started to cry.

Shit.

"We were wrong." Her father's voice was

thick. "So very wrong in how we treated you. And with the fire... You could have died and we just... we knew we had to talk to you. To set things right." He trailed off.

"You're not safe where you are," Bridget sniffed.

It was the last thing she'd expected them to say. "Excuse me?"

"Sit," Wallace said. "We need to tell you the truth about Val."

Delaney's tolerance for any more attacks on her aunt was running at near zero. But this had been a family mystery all her life. She'd at least sit through what they had to say.

Bridget got herself under control, mopping at the tears with the towel. "My sister and I used to be best friends. We were only a year apart. Two peas in a pod, we used to say. We even went to college together and shared an apartment. She loved taking me under her wing when I got there. Showing me around, intro-ducing me to people. But college was the first time I was exposed to a lot of different people. I started making my own friends and spending time with them. And then I met your father, and we fell in love."

Wallace picked up the story. "Val didn't take it well when we started spending all our time together. She was jealous and waspish."

"We had several fights about it. She kept telling me he wasn't who I thought he was. That he wasn't good for me. I didn't believe her."

I'm worried he's not good for you.

"She got desperate," her father said.

"Desperate?" Delaney repeated, hearing an echo of Sean's words from last night.

Wallace raked a hand through his hair, looking exceptionally uncomfortable. "She invited me out for drinks. Said it was to mend fences. She was there with one of her girlfriends, which was a little weird, but I didn't figure it was going to be a long conversation. We got our drinks, she started talking… and the next thing I knew, I was waking up in somebody else's bed with the friend, and your mom was standing in the doorway."

Delaney felt her face freeze. "I don't know if I need to know any more." The last image she needed in her head was her dad in bed with anybody, especially if that somebody wasn't her mother.

"Val drugged him and got her friend to agree to act like they'd slept together to 'prove' he was the terrible person she claimed he was. But the friend felt guilty and came and confessed after. She'd thought it was meant to be a funny prank and didn't feel right about how things actually happened. Your dad and I worked things out and confronted Val. And she went... crazy. I've never seen her so angry. She trashed our apartment, broke out the windows of my car, made threats. So, I left, and we cut her off."

"We had to," Wallace said. "She was... unhinged."

"We were scared, honey. She'd drugged your

father. She was violent toward me. The things she said, the way she saw things, it was like she wasn't seeing the same reality we were. She tried to manipulate me to see things her way, to manipulate the facts, and when I didn't, she couldn't stand that. Thinking about that time, I remember how scary it was. But I didn't want to remember that. And over time, I think what we really settled into was the anger and this idea that she was poison we wouldn't have in our lives."

The story was preposterous. Some kind of Machiavelli-meet-soap-opera insanity that bore no resemblance to the woman she knew. And it was coming from *her parents.* What motivation did they have to make up something this nuts? None, that she could think of. Certainly, if this was the truth, if Val had truly threatened and attacked them, the fact that they'd had nothing to do with her for years made a kind of sense.

Even as she accepted the logic of that, Delaney's gut twisted in realization of the parallels they must have drawn. She stared at her parents, feeling even more betrayed than she had when she got out of treatment. "So... when Bryce cheated on me and I lost it, you equated me to her... to *that?*"

"We didn't—" Wallace began.

"Yes," her mother whispered. "How could we not?"

"So, your answer to that was simply to cut me off, exactly like you did to her. Because you couldn't handle the fact that you have a daughter with problems."

Their eyes widened in shock. How could they be shocked? Was it just that she was finally calling them on the bullshit?

"We wanted you to come home so we could look after you. We told you that before you were released from the hospital," Wallace said.

Delaney bristled, remembering that one conversation. "You wanted to put me under house arrest. And that was after you came down on me like a ton of bricks for the trouble I got into over Bryce because you couldn't even fathom that I hadn't been in full control of my actions."

"Oh baby, no." Her mother started crying again. "I'm so ashamed that we didn't support you the way you needed during all that ugliness with Bryce. And maybe we didn't understand at first. Your behavior was so similar to Val's. But we didn't cut you off because you're bipolar. We had to cut you off because you chose Val."

"We told you if you made that choice, we couldn't have you in our lives," her father said. "Remember?"

Delaney frowned. No, she didn't remember. But she hadn't been a hundred percent leveled out when she got out of the hospital. It was possible things had gotten a little muddled in her head. That still didn't excuse their behavior for the past two years.

"I won't apologize for making that choice. I don't know what happened back then. I don't know Val's side of the story. What I do know is that I had a problem, and I needed help. Whatever mistakes Val made, she's more than made up for them. She gave me a home, support. She kept me from being out on the street when I got out of the hospital. She's never treated me like less. She's never treated me like I was broken. And she sure as hell has never walked away from me."

"That's the problem." Bridget reached out and laid a hand over Delaney's.

Delaney pulled her hand away.

"My therapist believes she's got borderline personality disorder. She... fixates on people, on her relationships with them. When we were young, it was me. Now it's you."

"You haven't been a part of my life for two years. How do you know anything about my relationship with Val?"

"Because I ran into her week before last. Right up the street from the community center. She told me off for how I treated you—and I deserved that. But she said I shouldn't worry because she was taking care of you the way we never did."

"That proves nothing but that she cares about me."

"Delaney, it was just minutes after Bryce's car was set on fire. We were less than a block away."

"That's coincidence. It's a small town. Why would she set Bryce's car on fire?"

"Because he hurt you. Because he brought all of it back up again and got Gina riled up against you."

Delaney shook her head and shoved back from the table. "I'm not listening to this."

"Honey, you have to," Wallace insisted. "Your aunt is very, very good at manipulating people, at making them see what she wants them to see. Until she gets pushed too far or doesn't get what she wants. She doesn't share the people she believes are hers."

"You're dating somebody new, right?" Bridget asked. "That new boy—the firefighter."

Delaney didn't bother to ask how she knew.

It was a small town. Everybody probably knew. And she didn't see the sense in explaining how they weren't together anymore.

"How has Val reacted to him?"

Jealous. Territorial. A ripple of unease rolled over her, a subtle chill beneath her other roiling emotions. Hadn't Delaney been worried about Val? Hadn't she known something wasn't quite as it should be?

"I have to go."

Ignoring her parents' protests, Delaney fled her childhood home. Everything they'd said whirled in her brain, mixing with the accusations Sean had made against her aunt. She'd get to the bottom of this. She'd simply get Val's side of the story. It couldn't be what it looked like.

But Val wasn't at the house when Delaney got there. Where the hell was she? Delaney needed answers. She paced the living room, the hall, trying to think. As her gaze fell on Val's bedroom door, Sean's words came back to her.

Search her room. If you find the money there, you'll have confirmation.

She had no right. But she needed to know. She needed to be able to throw the proof back in his face that he was wrong. So, she opened the door.

The room was neat. Her aunt was habitually organized. Delaney scanned the surface of the dresser, the nightstands. No envelope just obviously sitting out. Pushing aside the guilt, she began opening drawers, carefully sifting through the contents. And in the bottom of the underwear drawer, she found the envelope with all the donations from her friends.

"No." Her protest was barely a whisper as she sat down hard on the floor.

Val had stolen from her. Sean had been right about that. What if he was right about the rest? What if her parents had been telling nothing more than the truth?

Taking the envelope, Delaney rolled to her knees to rearrange the drawer as she'd found it. But there was more in here than the stolen money. Shifting a pile of bras aside, she pulled out another folded paper. It was a map. A smaller copy of the one Sean used to keep up with stuff for work. There were locations and dates scribbled on it. Was she *tracking* him?

Delaney knew little about borderline personality disorder, but if Val really had that kind of jealous attachment to her, what did that mean for Sean? Val didn't know they'd broken up. He'd said flat out, Val didn't like him and didn't like how he encouraged Delaney's independence. If she really had fixated on Delaney and had gone so far as to burn down the apartment to get her back into this house... what might she do to remove his influence?

"MAN, you aren't fit to be around people today. Take my shift in the fire tower. I'll make notes for the thinning. Hell, maybe Dunsford will actually listen if it comes from somebody other than you." Eli slapped the gate keys into Sean's hand.

Sean didn't argue. A night of little sleep had left him growly and short-tempered, with zero patience for dealing with the public and even less for passing more recs up the line to their boss that he'd only ignore. He appreciated that Eli didn't pry as to the source of his foul mood, as he gave a salute and got into the truck.

Six hours in total solitude would be good thinking time. He'd already decided last night that he needed to take his suspicions to the police. That was on the docket for after his shift. He was either right or wrong, and it would be in someone else's hands to prove. But he was still wrestling over what to do about Delaney. Apologize for how he handled things, certainly. But he didn't want things to be over between them, and he had no idea if she'd give him another chance.

Usually alone time in nature relaxed him, but an hour into his shift, Sean was still tense. His skin felt too tight, and the air seemed to drape over him like a wet blanket, despite the breeze that had the old tower swaying. The leaves on the surrounding trees rustled like paper in the wind, making him conscious of exactly how dry everything really was. A massive storm system was pushing its way across the state. It had originally been expected to hit Wachoxee County in the wee hours of the morning, but from this height, Sean could see the leading edge of it in the distance. They'd have some kind of action within an hour. If it dumped the kind of moisture they were expecting, it would be an end to the drought. But if it came with lightning, they'd still be at massive risk for fire. The idea of it made him twitchy. Much as he itched to fight the dragon, he didn't want to do it without a full team and resources. Mississippi wasn't equipped like the western states. Wildfires weren't the norm here, so they were ill prepared for future threats. Not that his boss had appreciated the reminders he'd been sending about that all summer.

The sound of tires on gravel had Sean swinging his gaze toward the narrow road leading up to the tower. The only person likely to come out here was Eli. Maybe he decided he wanted some of that alone time himself. Fine. Sean could go back to his original post for the afternoon. It sounded like he was coming awfully fast, though.

Frowning, Sean paced to the south side of the tower where he could watch for Eli's arrival. But it wasn't Eli's truck that skidded to a halt at the base of the tower. It was Delaney's car.

His pulse kicked up a few notches, but he didn't really believe it was her until he saw the flash of her hair as she slid out of the driver's side.

"Sean!"

Had she come all the way out here to yell at him some more?

"I'm here," he called.

She tipped her head back to look up, shielding her eyes from the glare of the early afternoon sun. "I need to talk to you."

"Come up. I'm on watch."

After a moment's hesitation, she let herself in through the gate and began to climb the stairs. By the time she made it to the top of the fifty-foot tower, she was winded.

"Here, have some water." He passed her a bottle, then curled his fingers into his palms to keep from touching her.

She took it with a flash of gratitude and gulped some down before gesturing with her other hand. "I didn't know these were still in use."

"They're not full time, but this summer, with the drought being so bad, I convinced my boss to press them back into service. How'd you find me?"

"You left your work schedule at the house. I followed it and found Eli. He sent me out here with orders to—and I quote— 'pull the stick out of your ass'." Her lips quirked. "I told him I'd give it my best effort."

The hint of a smile gave Sean hope. He still didn't know what to say to fix things, but he figured leading with an apology was never a bad tactic. "I'm sorry about yesterday. I'm sorry about what I said, how I said it. I'm sorry I put you in a position where you felt like you had to choose between me and family. I'm just sorry all the way around. I never intended to hurt you."

Delaney closed her eyes, something softening in her expression. "Thank you. I appreciate that." When she looked at him again, her blue eyes were serious. "There's so much I need to tell you, but before I get into that, I want to say I'm sorry, too, for how I reacted. I've got a sore spot, and you managed to stomp right on it. I didn't want to listen to anything you were saying because it felt like you were talking about me even though you weren't. It's so much the kind of shit I've been listening to for two years, and I just… didn't handle it well."

Sean took a step toward her and risked reaching out to nudge aside a strand of hair the wind blew across her face. "So, we're both sorry. Does this mean we maybe survived our first fight instead of breaking up?"

She stretched out a hand to his chest. "God, I hope so."

It was all the encouragement he needed to haul her against him and capture her mouth. Her arms twined around his shoulders, holding him tight, tight. She tasted of relief and heat and a sweetness he'd thought he'd never taste again. When his hands snaked under her shirt to skim up her back, she arched into the touch, then stiffened.

"Wait. Stop. Don't distract me. There's stuff I need to tell you."

"Unless it's of the 'Yes, Sean,' 'There,' 'More,' and 'oh, God, yes,' variety, I think it can wait." He underscored the point by kissing the tender spot below her ear that he knew made her go weak in the knees.

She gave a sexy little moan, fisting one hand in his shirt. "Oh, later. Definitely later. But I mean it. This is serious. You were right."

That had him going still. "About what?"

"My aunt. I went to see my parents this morning."

Well, that effectively killed his plans for makeup sex. "How did it go?"

"Not what you can call well."

Sean listened as she recounted the visit, and the family secret that had finally been spilled.

"I was so angry. At them. At you. I went home, determined to get Val's side of the story. But she wasn't there, and I had to have answers, so I searched her room, like you suggested. And I found the money."

He winced. "I'm sorry. I wish I hadn't been right."

"You can't be blamed for the truth."

Sean blew out a breath and took her hands in his. "Honey, we have to go to the police. If your mom really saw Val in the vicinity of that car fire, she needs to be looked at… hard."

Delaney closed her eyes. "I know."

"Let me see if I can get somebody to come cover the rest of my shift here. We'll drive on into town and get this over with. And then, I want you to think about packing and coming to stay with me. When Val gets confronted, she's not gonna take it well, and you don't need to be in the line of fire."

"Fair enough. But that's not what brought me out here. I also found this." She pulled a piece of folded paper from her pocket. "She *roofied my dad* and set him up in bed with someone else to try to split up my parents. If she's fixated on me the way my mom thinks, and she sees you as a threat... I don't know what she'll do. So, I came out here to warn you."

Sean opened the paper and felt the blood drain from his face.

"I wasn't sure exactly what it was, but there's absolutely no good reason for her to have this."

"It's the record I've been keeping all summer to track the areas of greatest fire threat in the region." He swallowed, scanning the notations she'd made beside his own. "If Val was behind all three fires, if she's gotten a taste for arson, then I've inadvertently handed her the key to starting the biggest wildfire the state has ever seen."

"Sean." Delaney's voice was choked.

"I know you don't want to think—"

"No, Sean, look!"

Her tone of alarm had him automatically shifting to shield her body with his as he turned and saw what she'd seen. A curl of smoke rising from the thick blanket of trees to the west.

CHAPTER 12

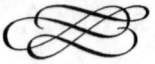

The truck bumped hard over the rutted road, jarring Delaney's teeth as Sean sped toward the fire. He'd been on the radio, reporting the blaze, giving coordinates, and asking for backup. All of it was a blur against the fear. He couldn't raise Eli on the radio. Eli, who was nearest the source of the fire. Exactly where Sean was supposed to be. Delaney was terrified about what they were going to find. Everything was so dry from the drought. Already the thin wisp of smoke had thickened against the cloudless blue of the sky. How far had it spread? How fast?

As he made a hard, skidding left onto another gravel road, Delaney prayed it wouldn't be Val and there was some other explanation, like some campers who were ignoring the burn ban. But when they passed Val's car, wedged against the brush at the shoulder of the road, she knew all hope was lost.

A little further on, Sean pulled the truck to the side and leapt out, already tugging on turnout gear.

"What are we going to do?" Delaney asked.

"You're going to stay here. I'm going in to do what I can to stop the spread." He hauled a massive chainsaw out of the truck bed.

"I'm not just going to sit here." The waiting would make her crazy.

"I don't have time to argue with you. It's not safe out there."

"We don't know what state Val's in. If she's desperate enough to do this, she might try to hurt you. If I go, maybe she'll listen to me."

Sean's eyes went hard as chips of jade. "If anything happens to you—"

"You think you're the only one who feels like that? I love you, and I won't let anything happen to you."

The rigid expression went slack with shock, and Delaney realized what she'd said. Too late to take it back now, and there was too much adrenaline in her system to be nervous about his reaction. "Let me just come with you to check. If she's not there, then I'll come right back to the truck. You said backup is en route, right?"

He growled and closed the distance between them, sliding a hand around her nape. "I love you, too." He kissed her, hard and fast. "We're gonna talk about that when this is over. Right now, you're going to come with me and see what there is to see. But if I tell you to go back, you go back. No questions, no argument. This whole goddamned forest is set to go up like a box of matches, and I don't want you caught in it."

Elated, terrified, Delaney could only nod and fall into step behind him as he picked up the saw and shouldered a massive pack bristling with tools. Sean's long strides ate up the ground, and she almost had to run to keep up. He seemed to look everywhere at once, analyzing conditions. For now, the wind was at their backs. She didn't know if that was a good or bad thing. Off in the distance, she could hear the rumble of thunder.

Rain. Rain would take the teeth out of the threat, surely. *Please, dear God, let the storm get here fast.*

The scent of smoke had a cold sweat trickling down Delaney's spine. It was too easy to remember being trapped in her burning apartment, unable to get out.

You're not trapped here. You can turn around at any time.

But she wouldn't turn around. Not until she knew where her aunt was and exactly what trouble she'd caused.

About a quarter mile in, the trees thinned

out, and Delaney could see the leap of flame. A bonfire had been built in the center of a small clearing. And standing a dozen feet away from it was Val, her expression rapt as she stared at what she'd built.

Delaney looked around, checking the trees above. So far, it didn't seem the fire had spread. But that wouldn't stay the case for long. Taking a step back, Val grabbed something off the ground and started to toss it into the fire.

"What the hell are you doing with my pack?" Sean demanded.

Val whipped around toward the sound of his voice, her hand extended toward the flames. Her eyes only went wider as he emerged from the trees in full turnout gear. She dropped the bag. It hit the edge of the bonfire.

"They'll find it and they'll know it was you."

"They'll know what was me?"

"The fire. You've spent all summer warning them of the dangers. They wouldn't listen. You miss your job as a hotshot, so you decided to start a little action yourself. Prove your point."

"Yeah, there's a problem with that scenario. You've just been caught red-handed."

"Who are they going to believe? You've got the map. You marked all the spots. It'll be enough to get you fired and sent away. You just need to go away so things can go back to normal."

Heart breaking, Delaney stepped into the clearing. "They're never going to go back to normal, Val."

Val's face went pale. "Delaney. What are you doing here?" She looked around, as if there was something she could do to hide what she'd done.

"Stopping you from making any more mistakes."

Her cheeks flushed with an unfamiliar rage. "Mistakes? I haven't made any mistakes. I've done everything for you. Gave you a home. Took care of you when your own parents turned their backs on you. Supported you. I even got revenge on those two assholes who ruined your life. And how do you thank me? You just keep pulling away. Abandoning me. For *him*."

"That wasn't my intention. But this... this is not okay. This isn't the way to keep me in your life."

"You'll leave me, just like your mother did. It's all his fault. I'm just trying to make him go away. If he goes away, things can be good again. We can be a family again."

Delaney took a step forward. "We're still family. We'll always be family. But Aunt Val, you need help, like I needed help."

The rage shifted to tears. "You think I'm crazy."

Another step toward her. "No. You're not crazy. I wasn't. You helped me understand that. I'd never have made the progress I have without you. Let me do for you what you did for me." Delaney closed the distance between them, wrapping her aunt in a hug. "I love you, and I'm sorry."

Val buried her face against Delaney's throat and wept.

"I need y'all to move back, so I can safely put this out." Sean's voice was calm, matter of fact.

Delaney dragged her aunt out of the way, focused on comforting her. By the time Val calmed down, Sean had dug a trench in a wide circle around the blaze and spread the burning branches so they'd burn out quicker. He moved fast and steady, shoveling dirt onto the flames.

The sound of someone tromping through the brush had Val tensing. Delaney tightened her grip, half afraid her aunt would bolt. A few moments later, Eli Hamilton emerged from the trees.

Oh, thank God, he was okay.

Eli took one look at the fire, then at Sean. "What the fuck, man?"

"Don't ask," Sean said. "You got that compact shovel in your pack?"

"Yeah."

"Pull it out and help me."

Eli stripped off his pack and set to work.

"Why the hell didn't you answer on the radio?" Sean asked.

"I was out at Cypress Bend and ended up helping an injured hiker. Left the radio in the truck, but I heard the traffic when I got back and came hustling. The crew's about fifteen minutes out. Should we call them off? This storm's nearly here."

Even as he said it, another growl of thunder rolled, close enough Delaney could feel the ground shake. She looked up to see the sky had gone dark, with angry-looking clouds. "Looks like we're probably gonna get wet."

"Better wet than dead," Sean said. "We're damned lucky this wasn't twenty yards north. Let's finish covering this thing, then we'll radio whoever hasn't—"

A bright bolt of lightning arced down from the sky not fifty feet away, crashing into the trees. The deafening crack of thunder drowned Delaney's scream.

"—everybody okay?" She saw rather than heard the words on Sean's lips. Her ears rang.

"I'm fine. I..." She trailed off as flames shot

high above the trees where the lightning had struck.

Sean whirled. "Fuck!"

In horror, Delaney watched as a gust of wind carried the sparks, like it was painting a canvas with orange in broad strokes. The fire leapt from tree to tree, the wood so dry, each one caught all but instantly, until a vibrant glow beat back against the darkness of the clouds. It was beautiful and terrible all at once, and as the wind shifted yet again, the fire seemed to writhe and rise before plunging in their direction like a creature crawling out of hell.

Sean scooped up his gear. "Eli, get them out of here. Direct the team to my location as soon as they arrive."

Eli grabbed his pack and swung toward Delaney and Val, already herding them back in the direction of the truck.

"Wait! What are you going to do?" Delaney called.

"Whatever I can. Go." Without another

word, he turned and ran right toward the mouth of the beast.

~

"Hot damn! I think we've knocked this bitch out!"

Sean could hear the adrenaline-laced elation in Hayden's voice and thought he might have the makings of a professional smoke eater. "Don't get cocky. She's not out yet."

Sean's one-man saw-line had barely made a dent to keep the dragon contained until help arrived. She'd spread farther and faster than he'd hoped, threatening to swallow them whole. But because he'd been studying this terrain for months, he'd known how to outsmart the beast. The responding units deferred to his experience—thank Christ—following orders for extending the line and trenching, so when the wind shifted and turned her head, she only had one direction to go. She'd burn out in another few hours. But how much more damage would she do in the meantime?

Grabbing up his chainsaw, he ignored the muscles screaming for rest and fuel and hustled along the flank, watching the sky for more lightning and praying they didn't get a fresh strike. *C'mon, Big Man, we could use an assist. You're just waiting up there with all that water. Let her loose.*

As if in response to his prayer, thunder rolled again, making the ground tremble. The sky opened up and dropped torrents of rain, soaking him to the skin in seconds. Tipping his head back and lifting his arms out to the side, he shouted, "Thank you!"

All around he heard the hiss and sizzle of fire being extinguished. Above it all rose a resounding cheer from the various crews of firefighters. This was the break they'd needed, the thing that would keep this contained instead of spreading out of control. But there was still work to be done. He hurried through the downpour to coordinate.

The teams stayed in place through the deluge, continuing their assigned tasks, tromping through the woods to make absolutely certain that every spark was out. It was well after dark by the time they finished cleanup and declared the dragon slain.

They'd been lucky. So damned lucky.

Sean didn't know exactly how many acres were lost. Close to a thousand by his estimation, but that information would come out tomorrow. There would be evaluations, reports, and decisions to be made about replanting. But most importantly, there'd been no loss of life, no loss of homes. For now, he was grateful it hadn't been worse. And so, it seemed, was his boss's boss. He had a meeting in Jackson with the head of the Forestry Commission to go over recommendations for better wildfire management.

But that was for later. Right this second, he wanted a shower, a beer, and an entire extra-large pizza from Speakeasy—possibly at the same time. But he needed to find Delaney.

As soon as he reached his truck, he called her.

"Hey. I saw on the news the fire was contained." There was relief in her voice, but also something else underneath.

"Yeah. We're done. Where are you?"

"Home." She sounded as exhausted as he felt.

"And Val?"

"With the police. I'll tell you about it when you get here."

"I'm on my way."

She met him at the door to Val's house, stepping toward him.

"Don't. I'm absolutely filthy."

"I absolutely don't care." She flowed into his arms, wrapping hers tight around him. "God, *God,* I was so afraid for you."

"I'm fine. It was just a baby dragon compared to what I fought out west. We got it under control."

"But it wouldn't have been, would it? If you hadn't been there when the lightning struck."

Longer response time, no limit to the food for the flames? "It would've been a lot worse."

She shuddered. "If we hadn't stopped Val, the lightning wouldn't have mattered."

"What happened?"

Stepping back, she towed him inside. "I'll tell you about it while you shower."

In the bathroom she started the spray, while he stripped out of his sodden clothes. With all the ash and mud, it was impossible to see what color they'd been. Delaney started to gather them up, but he stayed her hand. "No, leave them. I know what to do with them. Talk to me."

He stepped beneath the spray and lathered up.

"Once Eli got us back to the road, he was coordinating with the crew coming in to help you, so Val and I went back to her car. I drove us back to town. I convinced her it would go better for her if she reported what she'd done herself, like I did with the deck fire."

"The deck fire was a genuine accident. What your aunt did was not."

"No. But being cooperative can't hurt. So, we went in together and she confessed to everything."

"No attorney?"

"She's got one now. There's no way around her doing time. Not with multiple counts of arson. But I told her attorney to take the cooperation into account and to do whatever she could to push for a psych evaluation and treatment. She needs help, and I hope like hell she'll get it."

Hearing the heartache in her tone, Sean pulled the curtain back. "I'm sorry. I'm sorry you had to go through that with her alone. And I'm sorry it turned out like this."

"We're doing a lot of sorry today. I want to be done with sorry. I'll be there for her however I can through the trial and after. But I can't keep living my life worrying about her."

Reaching out, he stroked her cheek, wishing he could wipe away the pain. "Doesn't make you hurt any less."

She tipped her face into his hand. "No, it doesn't. And I'm sure I'll have some more bad days as we get through all this. But I want to move forward. I want to go to paramedic school. I want to help people. And I want you. More than anything else, I want you. You're my person, Sean."

"Your person?"

"My person. The one who gets me, like nobody else, and loves me anyway. And I want to be your person."

"You are." Heedless of the fact that he was soaking wet, and she was on the other side of the tub, he yanked her into him, wondering if she heard the rasp in his voice that wasn't just from eating smoke.

He wanted to take care of her in a million different ways, and her admission finally—*finally*—gave him the right to do that. The surety of being hers, of her being his, settled over him with a sense of everything falling into place. "I love you."

Delaney lifted her head and smiled. "Yeah, you said we'd talk about that."

Flashing her a grin, he pulled her fully into the shower and showed her instead. A million different ways, starting with the sexiest.

EPILOGUE

4 Months Later

*A*s her stomach gave a snarl, Delaney glanced at the clock. Ten after six. "What's taking so long?"

"Just one more patient to get out the door," Shelby announced. "Then pizza for all."

"We were waiting on test results," Piper explained. "Miranda's giving them now."

"What?" The shriek erupted from patient room two, echoing down the hall.

"I'm guessing they weren't good results." Delaney felt a pang of sympathy for whoever was in there.

Suddenly the door flew open. "—getting a second opinion. This is some kind of cruel joke. Payback for *her*."

Recognizing Gina Draper's strident voice, Delaney dropped down behind her desk before the other woman saw her. She didn't want another confrontation on her last day of work.

"You're welcome to seek a second opinion. But I assure you, it's no joke. This is a medical clinic, not a comedy club." Miranda's tone was firm. "Meanwhile, I suggest you have a conversation with your partner."

Oh, it was *that* kind of test result. Well, she was still with Bryce.

"You can be sure that I will. That son of a bitch is going to feel the business end of my stilettos."

"Before you go, I have a prescription for antibiotics. I realize this is upsetting news but fill it. Take the full course. For the sake of your own health."

Gina paused in her dramatic exit to settle the bill with Shelby. Delaney stayed where she was on the floor. She considered popping up to offer some unsolicited advice—*Do yourself a favor and dump his ass.* But she could feel the fury pumping off Gina in waves, and knew at the slightest provocation, she'd turn that on her. Better to stay put on the floor.

As soon as Gina was out the door, Piper locked it behind her.

Keisha pursed her lips. "Anybody else feel like that's a bit of karmic justice?"

"Keisha," Miranda warned.

"What? I'm just sayin'."

Miranda scooped both hands through her hair. "I'm going to call Ethan and warn him there's probably going to be a domestic disturbance tonight."

Delaney straightened from the floor. "Well, at least once I'm gone, you won't have to deal with that particular brand of drama again. Sorry she accused you of unprofessional conduct in my name."

"It's what I get for lifting the ban on her in the first place. Either way, we're gonna miss the hell out of you." Miranda gave her a squeeze.

"Oh, now, no getting maudlin yet," Piper warned. "There's pizza to be eaten!"

With long-practiced efficiency, they closed up the clinic and moved as a group over to Speakeasy for the official going away party. The place was packed, but for once, Delaney didn't hesitate to walk on in. Over the past few months, people had moved on from talking about her. There were other small town dramas taking center stage, and she seemed to have finally moved to the fringes of everybody's interest. As a whole, Wishful didn't really know or care that she was moving tomorrow. And that was exactly how Delaney wanted it. Everybody who did care congregated at the long table set up on the far side of the room.

Sean rose from his seat in the middle as she approached, that easy smile she so loved curving his lips. "Hey, babe. Good last day?"

Sliding into his arms, she lifted her face for

a kiss. "Getting better by the minute. Did y'all order yet?"

"Got some appetizers on the way. We figured y'all would be hungry." He pulled out a chair for her.

As she slid into it, she turned a smile on her parents across the table. "Glad you could make it."

"We wouldn't have missed it," her mom said.

Since Val's arrest, Delaney's parents had made a concerted effort to rebuild their relationship with her. It had been slow going. A lot of hurt feelings and misunderstandings lay between them all. But they'd gone out of their way to make sure she knew they didn't think of her as damaged. She was almost to the point of actually believing them.

They adored Sean. There hadn't even been raised eyebrows when they'd moved in together or when they'd announced they were moving to Jackson so Delaney could finish her paramedic training. Sean himself was taking a different position with the Mississippi Forestry Commission, advising the powers that be on preparedness for wildfires. They didn't expect it to turn into a permanent job, but it would be long enough for her to finish school. Then they'd explore their options for the next phase of their life. Delaney was past the point of questioning whether they'd still be together then. He was her rock. Period.

As her co-workers slipped into the remaining vacant seats, in between various members of the Wishful Volunteer Fire Department who'd turned out for the going away party, she wished Val could've been here. She'd been sentenced to two years at the Central Mississippi Correctional Facility. All in all, a conservative punishment considering the degree of her crimes. Delaney was doubly grateful to have been accepted into school in Jackson, as it would put her close enough to visit her aunt regularly, so that Val didn't feel so alone. She'd started therapy when she'd arrived at the prison. It was slow going, but at least she was finally somewhere she could get help.

Dinner was a boisterous affair, punctuated with stories and laughter and more pizza than it should've been possible to consume. By the time plates had been cleared and wine had been drunk, Delaney was relaxed and truly, all-the-way happy for the first time in longer than she could remember.

She tipped her head to Sean's shoulder. "Getting out of bed to load the truck tomorrow morning is going to take an act of Congress. I'm so full and sleepy."

"Consider it carb loading for the main event."

"Sure, we'll call it that," she chuckled.

"But we probably should be winding down. It's gonna be a long day."

A chorus of disappointment rose as they made their excuses.

"You *have* to come back to visit," Piper said.

"Yeah, keep us up to date on everything," Keisha added.

"I will do all of that. I promise." Delaney shoved back her chair and stood, immediately turning to start the goodbye hugging with Piper. "Oh, I'm gonna miss y'all so much!"

Miranda hugged her last. "I'm so proud of you. Even though you're going to be impossible to replace, and Shelby might explode the billing system as soon as you're gone."

"Hand to God, it will not be my fault," Shelby insisted. "Computers hate me. We know this. I swear you sacrificed a chicken every day to keep that thing running smoothly."

"Call me if you have problems. I'll walk you through it."

"Don't think I won't."

Delaney's ears were still ringing with well wishes as she and Sean stepped out of the pizzeria. She sucked in a lungful of the frigid December air. "Another chapter closed."

Sean tucked her close to his side. "Sad?"

"No. It's time to move on, and I'm good with it. It was nice to end on a high note."

"Walk with me a bit before we head home."

Willing to follow him anywhere, Delaney tucked her hand in his pocket and matched her stride to his. They crossed the street, strolling onto the town green. Everything was decked out for Christmas, with the town Christmas tree taking center stage in front of city hall. They made their way over to the quietly burbling fountain.

"Making a wish on your way out of town?" Delaney asked.

"Something like that." He stuck his hand into his pocket, bringing it out in a fist. "You want to make a wish?"

"I made mine already, back in the summer. I already got it, so I don't need to make another."

"Well, close your eyes while I make mine, anyway."

Game, she shut her eyes and heard Sean suck in a breath. His feet scraped on the sidewalk. She listened for the plunk of a coin but heard nothing.

"Okay," he said.

"I think you missed. I—" Words died on Delaney's tongue as she opened her eyes. Because

Sean was down on one knee, with a ring in his hand. "Ohmigod!"

He grinned up at her. "Tomorrow we're packing up all our stuff and moving on to the next big thing for both of us, and I wanted to do this here, tonight, before we left the place that brought us together. You're my person. So, I want to know, Delaney Christina Newell, if you'll marry me and make that official?"

Shock all but squeezed the breath out of her. "I—how did you know my middle name?"

"Your parents told me when I went to ask them."

"You asked my parents?"

"Preacher's kid. I'm an old-fashioned guy on some things. For what it's worth, they love me."

"So do I." She couldn't possibly measure how much.

"So, you wanna take this to the next level?"

"I absolutely do." Beaming, she reached for him, tugging him to his feet and into a kiss.

As his arms came around her, from somewhere behind them both, a chorus of cheers and whistles broke out.

"Called it!" Shelby shouted.

Laughing, Delaney broke the kiss. "We seem to have an audience."

"A complete entourage. You didn't think they were gonna miss out on this, did you?"

Looking over her shoulder, she saw everybody who'd been at dinner... and then some. Good God, had everybody in Speakeasy followed them out for this? She waited for the itch of discomfort at all the attention, the desire to scoot behind Sean and hide. But it didn't come. For once, she was the center of everybody's attention, and it was... awesome.

Sean pulled back enough to slip the ring on her finger—to more whooping and hollering.

She turned toward her friends and waved the new shiny. "They're gonna want to see. I say we give them ten minutes before we escape and head home to celebrate."

"Almost Mrs. Murphy, I like the way you think."

Choose Your Next Romance

If you're just discovering me through the Wishing For a Hero series, you may not know that I've got an entire series devoted to the lighter, happier side of Wishful. The Wishful Romance series is small-town, Southern romance at its finest, with all the big, interfering families, crazy octogenarians, and warm-fuzzies you could ask for. And more of those heroes who put their independent women first. Come visit Wishful, where hope springs eternal!

It begins with *To Get Me To You.*

OTHER BOOKS BY KAIT NOLAN

A complete and up-to-date list of all my books can be found at https://kaitnolan.com.

THE MISFIT INN SERIES
SMALL TOWN FAMILY ROMANCE

- *When You Got A Good Thing* (Kennedy and Xander)
- *Til There Was You* (Misty and Denver)

- *Those Sweet Words* (Pru and Flynn)
- *Stay A Little Longer* (Athena and Logan)
- *Bring It On Home* (Maggie and Porter)

RESCUE MY HEART SERIES
SMALL TOWN MILITARY ROMANCE

- *Baby It's Cold Outside* (Ivy and Harrison)
- *What I Like About You* (Laurel and Sebastian)
- *Bad Case of Loving You* (Paisley and Ty prequel)
- *Made For Loving You* (Paisley and Ty)

MEN OF THE MISFIT INN
SMALL TOWN SOUTHERN ROMANCE

- *Let It Be Me* (Emerson and Caleb)
- *Our Kind of Love* (Abbey and Kyle)

WISHFUL SERIES

SMALL TOWN SOUTHERN ROMANCE

- *Once Upon A Coffee* (Avery and Dillon)
- *To Get Me To You* (Cam and Norah)
- *Know Me Well* (Liam and Riley)
- *Be Careful, It's My Heart* (Brody and Tyler)
- *Just For This Moment* (Myles and Piper)
- *Wish I Might* (Reed and Cecily)
- *Turn My World Around* (Tucker and Corinne)
- *Dance Me A Dream* (Jace and Tara)
- *See You Again* (Trey and Sandy)
- *The Christmas Fountain* (Chad and Mary Alice)
- *You Were Meant For Me* (Mitch and Tess)
- *A Lot Like Christmas* (Ryan and Hannah)
- *Dancing Away With My Heart* (Zach and Lexi)

WISHING FOR A HERO SERIES (A WISHFUL SPINOFF SERIES)
SMALL TOWN ROMANTIC SUSPENSE

- *Make You Feel My Love* (Judd and Autumn)
- *Watch Over Me* (Nash and Rowan)
- *Can't Take My Eyes Off You* (Ethan and Miranda)
- *Burn For You* (Sean and Delaney)

MEET CUTE ROMANCE
SMALL TOWN SHORT ROMANCE

- *Once Upon A Snow Day*
- *Once Upon A New Year's Eve*
- *Once Upon An Heirloom*
- *Once Upon A Coffee*
- *Once Upon A Campfire*
- *Once Upon A Rescue*

SUMMER CAMP
CONTEMPORARY ROMANCE

- *Once Upon A Campfire*
- *Second Chance Summer*

ABOUT KAIT

Kait is a Mississippi native, who often swears like a sailor, calls everyone sugar, honey, or dar-lin', and can wield a bless your heart like a saber or a Snuggie, depending on requirements.

You can find more information on this

RITA ® Award-winning author and her books on her website http://kaitnolan.com. While you're there, sign up for her newsletter so you don't miss out on news about new releases!

www.ingramcontent.com/pod-product-compliance
Lightning Source LLC
Chambersburg PA
CBHW070523100726
47907CB00004B/963